You don't **HAVE** to read the Hiccup books in order.
But if you want to, this is the right order:

1. How to train your Dragon
2. How to be a Pirate
3. How to speak Dragonese
4. How to Cheat a Dragon's Curse
5. How to Twist a Dragon's Tale
6. A Hero's Guide to Deadly Dragons
7. How to Ride a Dragon's Storm
8. How to Break a Dragon's Heart
9. How to Steal a Dragon's Sword
10. How to Seize a Dragon's Jewel
11. How to Betray a Dragon's Hero
12. How to Fight a Dragon's Fury

JOIN HICCUP ON HIS QUEST
(although he doesn't quite realise he is on one yet...)

THE PROPHECY OF
THE KING'S LOST THINGS

'The Dragontime is coming
And only a King can save you now.
The King shall be the
Champion of Champions.

You shall know the King
By the King's Lost Things.
A fang-free dragon, my second-best sword,
My Roman shield,
An arrow-from-the-land-that-does-not-exist,
The heart's stone, the key-that-opens-all-locks,
The ticking-thing, the Throne, the Crown.

And last and best of all the ten,
The Dragon Jewel shall save all men.'

HICCUP the Hero of this Story

TOOTHLESS Hiccup's disobedient little dragon

Hiccup's best friend FISHLEGS

STOICK THE VAST Hiccup's father and chief of the Hooligan Tribe (tough but dim)

HORRORCOW Fishlegs's dragon

MUM

SNOTLOUT

op of the class at
ashyball, Advanced
dery. Senseless Violence
nd everything else

DOGSBREATH
THE DUHBRAIN
Snotlout's friend + fellow bully

FIREWORM
Snotlout's dragon

ALVIN
a Poor-But-Honest
Farmer
teacher in charge
of the Pirate
Training Programme

GOBBER
THE
BELCH →

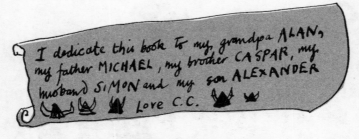

I dedicate this book to my grandpa ALAN, my father MICHAEL, my brother CASPAR, my husband SIMON and my son ALEXANDER Love C.C.

A big thank you to Simon Cowell, Caspar Hare, Tiina Jalava and Andrea Malaskova for all their hard work and support

HODDER CHILDREN'S BOOKS

First published in Great Britain in 2004 by Hodder & Stoughton
This edition published in 2017 by Hodder & Stoughton

7 9 10 8

SPECIAL EDITION

ISBN: 978-1-444-93552-3

Cover design by Jennifer Stephenson
Background cover illustration by Christopher Gibbs

Printed and bound by Clays Ltd, St Ives Plc

The paper and board used in this book are made from wood from responsible sources.

Hodder Children's Books
An imprint of Hachette Children's Group, Part of Hodder & Stoughton
Carmelite House, 50 Victoria Embankment, London EC4Y 0DZ
An Hachette UK Company
www.hachette.co.uk

How to Be a Pirate

written and illustrated by

CRESSIDA COWELL

Hodder
Children's
Books

A division of Hachette Children's Group

In the summer of 2002, a boy digging on a beach found a box that contained the following papers.

They are the lost second volume of memoirs of Hiccup Horrendous Haddock the Third, the famous Viking Hero, Dragon-Whisperer and Top Swordfighter.

They tell the story of how he acquired his famous sword, his first meeting with his arch-enemy The Most High and Murderous Chief of the Outcasts, and the terrible secret of the Treasure of Grimbeard the Ghastly...

~ CONTENTS ~

Not to Scale

N

W   E

S

The Outcast Lands

The
Peaceable
Country

There be
TREASURE
at the
Death's Head.

Isle of Berk

Meathead Islands

1. SWORDFIGHTING AT SEA (BEGINNERS ONLY)

Thor was SERIOUSLY annoyed.

He had sent a mighty summer storm to claw up the seas around the bleak little Isle of Berk. A black wind was shrieking across the wild and angry ocean. Furious thunder boomed overhead. Lightning speared into the water.

Only a madman would think it was the kind of weather for a pleasant sail.

But, amazingly, there was *one* ship being hurled violently from wave to wave, the hungry ocean chewing at her sides, hoping to tip her over and swallow the souls aboard and grind their bones into sand.

The madman in charge of this ship was Gobber the Belch. Gobber ran the Pirate Training Programme on the Isle of Berk and this crazy voyage was, in fact, one of Gobber's lessons, Swordfighting at Sea – (Beginners Only).

'OK, YOU DRIPPY LOT!' yelled Gobber, a six-and-a-half-foot hairy muscle-bound lunatic, with a beard like a ferret having a fit and biceps the size of your head. 'PUT YOUR BACKS INTO IT, FOR THOR'S SAKE. YOU ARE NOT AN ICKLE PRETTY JELLYFISH... HICCUP, YOU ARE ROWING LIKE AN EIGHT-YEAR-OLD... THE FAT BIT OF THE OAR GOES IN THE WATER... WE HAVEN'T GOT ALL YEAR TO GET THERE...' etc. etc.

Hiccup Horrendous Haddock the Third gritted his teeth as a big wave came screaming over the side and hit him full in the face.

Hiccup is, in fact, the Hero of this story, although you would never have guessed this to look at him. He was on the small side and had the sort of face that was almost entirely unmemorable.

There were twelve other boys struggling with the oars of that ship, and practically all of them looked

more like Viking Heroes than Hiccup did.

Wartihog, for instance, was only eleven, but he already had a fine crop of bubbling adolescent pimples and a personal odour problem. Dogsbreath could row as hard as anybody else with one hand, while picking his nose with the other. Snotlout was a natural leader. Clueless had ear hair.

Hiccup was just absolutely average, the kind of unremarkable, skinny, freckled boy who was easy to overlook in a crowd.

Beneath the rowing benches, thirteen dragons were huddled, one for each boy.

The dragon belonging to Hiccup was much, much smaller than the others. His name was Toothless, an emerald green Common or Garden dragon with enormous eyes and a sulky expression.

He was whining to Hiccup in Dragonese.*

'These Vikings c-c-crazy. Toothless g-g-got salt in his wings. Toothless sitting in a big cold puddle. Toothless h-h-hungry... F-F-FEED ME.' He tugged at Hiccup's trousers. 'Toothless need f-f-food NOW.'

a dragon's wings make a great umbrella...

---

*Dragonese was the native tongue of the dragons. I have translated it into English for the benefit of those readers whose Dragonese is a bit rusty. Only Hiccup could understand this fascinating language.

19

'I'm sorry, Toothless,' Hiccup winced as
the boat plunged maniacally downwards on the
back of another monstrous wave, 'but this is not
a good moment...'

'THOR ONLY KNOWS,' yelled Gobber,
'how you USELESS LOT got initiated into the tribe
of the Hairy Hooligans… but you now face four tough
years on the Pirate Training Programme before you can
truly call yourselves VIKINGS.'

Oh great, thought Hiccup gloomily.

'We will begin with the most important
Viking Skill of all… SWORDFIGHTING AT SEA.'
Gobber grinned.

'The rules of Pirate Swordfighting are…
THERE ARE NO RULES. In this lesson, biting,
gouging, scratching and anything else particularly
nasty all get you extra points. The first boy to call out
"I submit" shall be the loser.'

'Or we all drown,' muttered Hiccup, 'whichever
is the sooner.'

'NOW,' shouted Gobber. 'I NOMINATE
THE FIRST BOY AS DOGSBREATH THE
DUHBRAIN. WHO'S GOING TO FIGHT HIM?'

Dogsbreath the Duhbrain grunted happily at the

thought of spilling blood. Dogsbreath was a mind-less thug of a boy with hairy knuckles that practically grazed the ground as he walked, and mean little eyes and a big ring in his flared nostrils made him look like a bristly boar with a bad character.

'Who shall fight Dogsbreath?' repeated Gobber the Belch.

Ten of the boys stuck their hands up with cries of '*Oooosirmesirpleasechoosemesir,*' wildly excited at the thought of being smooshed into a pulp by Dogsbreath the Duhbrain. This was predictable. That's what most Hooligans were like.

But what was more surprising was that HICCUP also leapt to his feet shouting, 'I nominate myself, Hiccup Horrendous Haddock the Third!'

This was unusual because while Hiccup was
the only son of Chief Stoick the Vast, he was not what
you might call 'naturally sporty'. He was nearly as bad
at Bashyball, Thugger, and all the other violent Viking
games as his best friend Fishlegs.

And Fishlegs had a squint, a limp, numerous
allergies and no co-ordination whatsoever.

'What has got into you?' whispered Fishlegs.
'Sit down, you lunatic... He'll murder you...'

'Don't worry, Fishlegs,' said Hiccup, 'I know
what I'm doing here.'

'OK, HICCUP,' boomed Gobber in surprise.
'Get up here, boy, and show us what you're made of.'

'If I'm EVER going to be Chief of this Tribe,'
whispered Hiccup to Fishlegs, as he started taking off
his jacket and buckling on his sword, 'I'm going to
have to be a Hero at *something*...'

'Trust me,' said Fishlegs, 'THIS IS NOT YOUR
THING... Clever ideas, yes. Talking to dragons, yes.
But one-to-one combat with a brute like Dogsbreath?
Absolutely NO, NO, NO.'

Hiccup ignored him. 'The Horrendous Haddocks
have always had a gift for swordfighting. I reckon it's
in the blood... Look at my great-great-grandfather,

Grimbeard the Ghastly. Best
swordfighter EVER...'

'Yes, but have YOU ever done any
swordfighting before?' asked Fishlegs.

'Well, no,' admitted Hiccup, 'but I've read
books on it. I know all the moves... The Piercing
Lunge... The Destroyer's Defence... Grimbeard's
Grapple... And I've got this great new sword...'

The sword was, indeed, an excellent one,
a Swiftpoint Scaremaker with go-faster stripes and
a handle shaped like a hammerhead shark.

'Besides,' said Hiccup, 'I'm never going to be
in actual danger...'

The Pirates-in-Training practised with wooden
cases on their swords. 'Molly-coddling, we never did
that in MY DAY,' was Gobber's opinion. However,
it DID mean the Hooligan Tribe ended up with more
live Pirates at the end of the Programme.

Fishlegs sighed. 'OK, you madman. If you have to
do this... keep looking in his eyes... keep your sword
up at all times... and say a big prayer to Thor the
Thunderer because you're going to need all the help
you can get...'

Swiftpoint Scaremaker

2. THE FIGHT WITH DOGSBREATH THE DUHBRAIN

Dogsbreath stood, pawing the deck in anticipation.

'KILL HIM, DOGSBREATH!' shouted Snotface Snotlout, Dogsbreath's friend and fellow bully.

Snotlout LOATHED Hiccup.

'I will,' grinned Dogsbreath.

'This will be a massacre,' hissed Dogsbreath's dragon Seaslug, an ugly great Gronckle with a pug nose and a mean temper. 'My master will tear this Hiccup limb from limb and throw him to the gulls.'

'D-d-don't bet on it,' said Toothless, without a lot of conviction, and he gave Seaslug a sharp nip on the tail before scrambling for cover underneath one of the rowing benches.

Hiccup edged forward towards the hulking figure of Dogsbreath, swallowing hard. He tried to remember what The Hero's Handbook had said about swordfighting an opponent much bigger than yourself... Something about ducking about, letting the enemy exhaust himself, using his own

Dogsbreath the Duhbrain

body weight against him…

'D-d-don't let him c-c-catch you!' advised
Toothless, appearing for a moment from underneath
the bench and then diving back into his hiding-place as
Seaslug lunged at him with a crunching crash of razor-
sharp teeth.

Hiccup stepped forward lightly and calmly, looking
Dogsbreath straight in the mean, piggy little eyes.

Dogsbreath grinned nastily at him, and aimed
a huge flailing swipe at his head.

Hiccup ducked.

'Yay, HICCUP!' cheered Fishlegs. 'That's the way
to do it!'

Dogsbreath looked rather surprised. He swiped
at Hiccup again, even more violently.

And again Hiccup ducked.

This time he was so quick about it that
Dogsbreath staggered and nearly lost his footing.

'HIC-CUP! HIC-CUP! HIC-CUP!' yelled most of
the boys. (Hiccup was popular with the other
boys at the time because a month before he had
single-handedly killed a Sea Dragon that threatened the
whole Tribe.)*

---

*See *How to Train Your Dragon,* the first volume of Hiccup's memoirs.

I can Do this

Hiccup felt a little bubble of happiness somewhere inside him.

This was great.

Now Dogsbreath was getting cross. He snorted furiously, and lunged forward straight at Hiccup's heart. Hiccup dodged nimbly out of the way and... slipped on a slimy piece of the deck and... Dogsbreath reached out one meaty fist and... grabbed Hiccup by the back of the shirt and caught him.

This was not so great.

OK, thought Hiccup. *So he's caught me. What do I do now then?*

Toothless burst out from underneath the bench and hovered for a second or two, three inches from Hiccup's nose, shrieking, 'S-S-SUBMIT! S-S-SUBMIT! S-S-SUBMIT!' at the top of his voice before zooming back to safety.

'I can't submit,' said Hiccup indignantly.

'I'm supposed to be this Pirate Hero. Pirates don't submit.'

'Oh goodee,' said Dogsbreath happily before whacking Hiccup briskly on the helmet a few times with his sword. Hiccup tried to stop him, but each time he was too slow to protect himself.

This is just embarrassing, thought Hiccup as Dogsbreath's sword clanged off his helmet for the third time. *Time to try a few moves.*

He had a go at the Destroyer's Defence. He could see himself in his mind's eye, elegant, stylish. But when his brain tried to tell his arm what to do, his arm responded in this clumsy, fumbling way, and Dogsbreath grabbed hold of the fancy Swiftpoint Scaremaker and threw it over the side into the ocean.

There were hoots and jeers from the watching Vikings.

Fishlegs and Toothless winced. 'Toothless can't l-l-look,' moaned Toothless, with his wings over his eyes. 'S-S-SUBMIT, you stupid human.'

29

'What are you going to do, Hiccup?' sneered Snotlout. 'Fight him with your bare hands? Or SUBMIT?'

'No way,' said Hiccup stubbornly.

Dogsbreath moved in for the kill with a few breath-quenching jabs to the stomach. 'Oh for THOR'S SAKE, Hiccup,' yelled Gobber in exasperation. 'You're fighting like an infant. You're not going to get anywhere by lying on the floor groaning. Bite him on the ankle or SOMETHING.'

'He's USELESS,' crowed Snotlout gleefully. 'Hiccup the Useless, didn't I tell you? All that Dragon-Killing last month was just a fluke. USE-LESS, USE-LESS, USE-LESS...'

Boys are very fickle. Hiccup's popularity vanished on the spot. They started chanting 'USE-LESS, USE-LESS, USE-LESS...'

The dragons joined in eagerly.

'Scratch his eyes out!' screeched Brightclaw.

'Tear his wings off!' howled Fireworm.

'S-s-submit,' moaned Toothless.

With a snort of satisfaction, Dogsbreath threw away his own sword and got down to the business he really enjoyed, hand-to-hand combat. Dogsbreath was an artist in his own sweet way. He liked to get the feel of his victim's flesh in his bare hands, like a sculptor with his clay.

Dogsbreath began by sitting on Hiccup, to the huge cheers of the rest of the boys. He followed this by scrunching Hiccup's face into the deck and twisting his ear at the same time.

'Oh suffering scallops,' said Fishlegs, shutting his eyes. 'I can't watch this. YOU CAN STILL DO IT HICCUP!' he shouted. 'USE HIS BODY WEIGHT AGAINST HIM!'

'And just how,' enquired Hiccup out of one corner of his mashed mouth, 'am I supposed to do that with him sitting on top of me?'

While everybody was concentrating on watching this massacre, Snotlout sneakily picked up Dogsbreath's sword and removed the wooden case.

'SUBMIT! SUBMIT! SUBMIT!' yelled Dogsbreath, gleefully bouncing up and down.

'No,' said Hiccup.

'Maybe ickle Hiccup is going to start cwying,' crowed Snotlout.

'USE-LESS, USE-LESS, USE-LESS,' chanted the boys.

It was too tempting...

Toothless emerged from beneath Wartihog's bench. He looked left and right for any sign of Seaslug. And there, only inches away, was Dogsbreath's gigantic quivering bottom. It was too tempting. Toothless unlocked his jaws as wide as they would go.

As his name suggests, Toothless was entirely fang free. But his hard little gums could slice through the shell of an oyster and crush the claws of a crab...

He leapt forward and BIT that wobbling rear-end as hard as he could.

'OOOOOOOW!' howled Dogsbreath, letting go of Hiccup, who scrambled out of his way as quickly as he could.

Now Dogsbreath was really *really* mad.

He grabbed hold of his sword, not realising or caring that it no longer had a wooden case on it, and lunged wildly at Hiccup. Hiccup leapt out of the way, but the sharp point of the blade pierced his shirt and tore a neat slice out of it.

'Uh-oh,' said Hiccup, suddenly realising he was in Big Trouble. 'Dogsbreath, your sword has lost its...'

But Dogsbreath wasn't listening. He gave a roar of maddened fury, and made a great slashing swipe at

Hiccup's head. Hiccup ducked and the wickedly sharp blade buried itself in the mast of the boat, slicing the top off one of the horns on Hiccup's helmet in the process.

'STOP!' cried Hiccup from behind the mast, as Dogsbreath tugged furiously at his sword to pull it free. 'Your sword has lost its case, you're going to KILL ME...'

But Dogsbreath was so angry he could not hear a thing. He gave a great heave with his mighty muscles and the sword jerked free so suddenly that the poor brute sat down heavily on his bottom, just on that tender spot where Toothless had taken a big chunk out of it.

'YOOOOOOOOOW!' yelled Dogsbreath.

'HA HA HA HA HA!' laughed the boys.

Dogsbreath staggered to his feet, as mad as a harpooned whale. He threw himself at Hiccup with great bellows of fury. Although Hiccup managed to avoid him again, this time he slipped over in the process. Dogsbreath pinned him down with one giant hand, and he lifted his sword above his head with the other.

'DON'T DO IT!' shouted Hiccup desperately, but Dogsbreath's eyes were full of the joys of battle and he began to swing the blade down towards Hiccup's chest.

And that would have been the end of Hiccup if it hadn't been for the extraordinarily lucky coincidence that at that very moment the ship lurched queasily upwards on the next giant wave, rolled for a second on the brim, and plunged hysterically downwards… straight on to a large floating object that instantly holed the boat.

'Abandon ship!' shrieked Fireworm, and thirteen dragons rose into the air like gigantic bats. (Dragons are only loyal to their Masters up to a certain point.)

The ship split into two pieces on the spot, spilling the Vikings out into the sea. It then sank, with a sigh of relief, to the bottom of the ocean bed in about ten seconds flat.

One minute Hiccup was in the not-so-loving embrace of Dogsbreath the Duhbrain, the next he was doing the doggy paddle in water so breath-quenchingly, spine-numbingly, heart-stoppingly cold that it was difficult to think of questions like: 'What in Woden's name do we do now?'

Something landed with a bump on the top of Hiccup's helmet. Toothless's eyes peered into his, upside down.

'N-n-nice fighting, Master,' he said. 'N-n-now,

where's my l-l-lunch?'

'You may not have noticed,' said Hiccup, swallowing a big chunk of seawater as the weight of Toothless pushed him under the surface, 'but I'm having a bit of a crisis here. Now flap off, will you, and see what's happened to Fishlegs, he can't swim.'

Hiccup *could* swim but the waves were mountainously rough. He really had to struggle to keep afloat.

Toothless returned a moment or so later looking anxious.

'F-f-fishlegs d-d-definitely needs your help Master. B-b-big trouble. Follow me.'

And he disappeared again.

Hiccup was just thinking, 'Well I don't know what in Valhalla he thinks I can do about it,' when a miracle occurred.

3. A CHANCE IN A MILLION

The object that had holed the boat, thereby saving
Hiccup from Death at the hands of Dogsbreath
the Duhbrain, was a large, heavy, six foot by three
foot BOX.

It now floated up to within reaching distance
of where Hiccup was treading water. There were a
couple of iron handles on the sides, very handy for
grabbing on to.

About twenty minutes earlier, some laughing
members of the Meathead Tribe had thrown this box
into the sea at Meathead Island, which was a couple
of miles away. The winds had carried it a considerable
distance in that short time.

And the chances of that particular box travelling
all that way, and then in the middle of the whole wild
and lonely ocean happening to hole the ship just in
time to save Hiccup's life, must have been thousands,
no, millions to one.

If you were a fanciful person, you might have
said that it was almost as if that box was *looking*
for Hiccup.

But we are not fanciful people, and that would be ridiculous.

No sooner had Hiccup grabbed hold of one of the iron handles with a sigh of relief, than a gigantic wave lifted him and the box way, way up, and then deposited them crashing down only a couple of feet away from where Toothless was trying to keep Fishlegs from going under for the third and what would have been final time.

The dragon had a firm grip on the back of Fishlegs's shirt, his wings were flapping furiously, and his little green face had turned bright red with the effort of trying to stop Fishlegs from sinking.

Fishlegs had got hold of a piece of broken oar that was keeping him up a bit, but he couldn't cling on much longer, and he would have drowned if it had not been for the sudden arrival of Hiccup and the mysterious box.

There was a lull in the sea for a couple of moments, in which Hiccup and Toothless managed to heave the exhausted Fishlegs on to the top of the box.

And there he clung, like an anxious Daddy-Long-Legs, terrified but alive.

Five indescribably cold minutes later, they were

blown by the violence of the wind on to the shores
of the Long Beach. Amazingly, all thirteen of the
boys and Gobber himself had survived the shipwreck.

Gobber didn't exactly give them a big,
welcoming hug.

'Mmmm, good work I suppose,' he said begrudg-
ingly, sniffing a bit. 'You took your time about it,
though. Step lively, Fishlegs. We're horribly late for the
next lesson.'

As soon as Fishlegs had dragged himself off
the box, and collapsed panting on to the beach,
Gobber stopped being irritated.

Because the box wasn't a box at all.

It was a coffin.

A huge, six-and-a-half-foot floating coffin,
with the following words carved into the lid:

4. WHOSE COFFIN IS THIS ANYWAY?

The boys all crowded around the box, forgetting, in their curiosity, about their narrow escape from drowning.

'It's a coffin, sir.'

'Yes, I can see that, thank you, Wartihog,' snapped Gobber the Belch. 'The question is, whose?'

The answer was written right underneath the words 'Do Not Open This Coffin', in letters scratched out with some kind of dagger, and stained with something that might once have been blood.

'CURSED BE HE WHO DISTURBS THE REMAINS OF GRIMBEARD THE GHASTLY THE GREATEST PIRATE WHO EVER STRUCK TERROR INTO THE INNER ISLES.'

Hiccup felt a cold clammy shiver run down his back, and he suddenly knew that something really bad was going to happen.

Grimbeard the Ghastly had been Hiccup's own great-great-grandfather.

'The Lost Treasure of Grimbeard the Ghastly' was a popular Hooligan Saga. It told of how

Grimbeard had won a glorious treasure through his brilliance at piracy and swordfighting, a treasure that included his famous sword, the Stormblade.

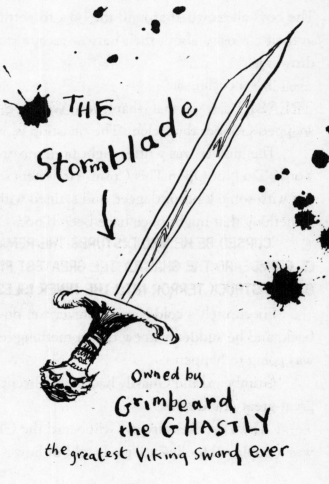

THE Stormblade

Owned by Grimbeard the GHASTLY
the greatest Viking sword ever

But after twenty years of glorious rule, Grimbeard had disappeared on a mysterious quest, and neither he nor the treasure were ever seen again.

And now here, out of the blue, one hundred years later, his coffin had appeared back on the shores of Berk... It was spooky.

'OOOOOOOH,' chattered Wartihog in excitement. 'Do you think there might be TREASURE in there, sir? Can we open it, sir? Pleasesir, pleasesir, can we open it?'

All the other boys joined in the clamour... except for Hiccup.

Hiccup knew that Grimbeard had been the ULTIMATE in pirate-ness, the GREEDIEST, GRISLIEST, GORIEST Viking who had ever sailed and slew and farted his way across the Northern Seas.

Treasure or no treasure, if a man like Grimbeard the Ghastly was telling you not to mess with his coffin, it was Hiccup's personal opinion that you ought to listen.

Even if he had been dead for a hundred years.

Particularly if he had been dead for a hundred years.

'Right,' said Gobber, just as excited as everybody

else, 'we're going to have to forget about the Advanced Rudery lesson. This is an Important Discovery and I think we should take it straight to Stoick the Vast and the Council of Elders. Bearhug, Sharpknife, Wartihog, Clueless, pick it up and carry it back to the Hooligan Village...'

The boys hauled the coffin on to their shoulders.

'Don't just hang about shivering, you lazy lug-fish,' Gobber bellowed crazily. 'This is Pirate Training, not a holiday with your mother on the Mainland. QUICK MARCH, one-two, one-two, one-two...'

He set off at a brisk trot towards the Hooligan Village.

The boys sighed and began to stumble after him.

Snotlout and Dogsbreath the Duhbrain sauntered over to Hiccup, who was sitting trying to catch his breath on a large rock, shivering violently.

'A shame that Dogsbreath was interrupted,' sneered Snotlout, 'just when things were getting interesting, don't you think, Dogsbreath?'

'Yeah,' grinned Dogsbreath the Duhbrain.

'I reckon,' said Snotlout thoughtfully to the remaining boys, 'that Hiccup must be the most pathetic swordfighter I have EVER seen, don't you think, guys? I mean, face it, Hiccup, somebody who fights like a granny with a back problem is NEVER going to be Chief of this Tribe...'

'Oh, and so who *is* going to be Chief of this Tribe if Hiccup isn't?' asked Fishlegs, still lying spreadeagled on the sand in the exact position where he had fallen off the coffin. 'Let me guess... YOU, I suppose?'

Snotlout flexed his muscles, making the skeleton tattooed on his right bicep grin smugly.

'I AM the obvious choice,' he said. 'I've got noble blood...' (Snotlout was Hiccup's cousin, the son of Baggybum the Beerbelly, the Chief's younger brother) 'charisma... good looks...' (Snotlout stroked the rather unpleasant little straggly hairs on his upper lip that he was trying to grow into a moustache) '... and I'm BRILLIANT at absolutely everything...'

Unfortunately this was true.

Snotlout was a natural at Mindless Violence, superb at Advanced Rudery and practically everything else.

'... particularly swordfighting,' said Snotlout, drawing his sword from its scabbard.

The other boys gasped.

The Latest Double-Sided Extra-Biting Supa-Sword (like Snotlout's Flashcut)

'Wow,' breathed Speedifist. 'The latest Double-Sided Extra-Biting Supa-Sword. Curving inner edges, silverpoint finish... where did you get THAT from, Snotlout?'

'This is the Flashcut,' boasted Snotlout, swishing the beautiful sword around so that everybody could get a good look. 'Makes that silly Swiftpoint Scaremaker that Dogsbreath lost for you look pretty weak, doesn't it, Hiccup? Let me show you how Swordfighting should be done. This,' sneered Snotlout, lunging athletically, 'is a Perfect Pointer...'

Hiccup dodged.

'And this is the Destroyer's Defence...' Snotlout gave an animal howl and brought the sword down over his head, stopping just before he cut Hiccup in half.

'And that,' jeered Snotlout, slashing the Flashcut expertly from side to side and then leaping forward suddenly, the sword ending up just inches away from Hiccup's heart, '*that* is a Grimbeard's Grapple...

46

But I expect a loser like you, who couldn't even beat a three-year-old in nappies, hasn't even *heard* of moves like that.'

Hiccup said nothing.

'THAT, dear cousin,' sneered Snotlout, 'is HOW TO SWORDFIGHT.' He put his sword back in its scabbard.

'Yup,' he said, very pleased with himself, 'I'm a genius. I'm going to make the best Chief this Tribe has ever had.'

'It's just a shame,' said Fishlegs, 'that your brain isn't as big as one of your nostrils.'

Snotlout looked irritated for a second as all the other boys laughed. He grabbed Hiccup by the scruff of the neck and lifted him clear off the ground.

'Amazing how the wooden case to that sword fell off, wasn't it?' he spat right into Hiccup's face. 'You were lucky this time… but the question is, can you be lucky ALL the time? Think about it, LOSER. Come on, Dogsbreath. Let's leave the girlies to get their beauty sleep.'

He dropped Hiccup and as he went he trod heavily and deliberately on one of Fishlegs's hands. 'Whoops,' laughed Snotlout.

'Har Har Har Har,' snorted Dogsbreath the Duhbrain.

And they jogged off.

'If Snotlout is EVER Chief of this Tribe, I'm emigrating,' said Fishlegs, shaking his hand.

'Are you all right, Fishlegs?' asked Hiccup with concern, as he gazed down on Fishlegs still lying flat on his back.

'Perfect,' croaked Fishlegs, coughing up a bit more seawater. 'I do love an early morning swim. How about you?'

'Oh, couldn't be better really,' said Hiccup bleakly, taking off one of his boots and pouring out a flood of seawater and a couple of small fish.

'My first day at Pirate Training and I've already been humiliated by my pathetic swordfighting, beaten to a pulp, shipwrecked, and narrowly escaped Death by drowning. And it's not even ten o'clock yet.'

'Maybe it was the SWORD that was the problem,' suggested Fishlegs kindly but untruthfully.

Hiccup brightened up.

'You could be right,' he said eagerly, 'it felt a bit light in my hands. Perhaps I need something a bit chunkier, you know, to get some weight behind my swing.' He did a few imaginary lunges in the air. 'That must be it, because I still have this feeling that swordfighting is going to be my thing, you know?'

'Um, yeeeessss,' said Fishlegs, not wanting to hurt Hiccup's feelings by mentioning that it had been the worst display of swordfighting he had seen, EVER. 'And you need a lot more PRACTICE, don't you think?'

Hiccup nodded enthusiastically. 'Anyway,' he said, 'we need to get after the others. I'm freezing, and I've a horrible feeling that some idiot is going to suggest OPENING that coffin which says quite clearly DO NOT OPEN. It would be just the sort of mindlessly stupid thing they would do.'

'What do you think could be in it?' asked Fishlegs.

'I don't know,' said Hiccup, 'but a pirate like Grimbeard the Ghastly won't have hidden the treasure in it without booby-trapping it in some way. You read what it said on the top... A man like him could have thought of all SORTS of unpleasant surprises.'

Fishlegs sighed and struggled to his feet. They set off slowly towards the Hooligan Village, Toothless hitching a ride on Hiccup's helmet.

'They wouldn't open it, would they?' worried Fishlegs. 'Surely, surely, SURELY, they couldn't be that stupid?'

Grimbeard the GHASTLY

5. DO NOT OPEN a coffin that says 'DO NOT OPEN' on the front

As soon as they got to the Hooligan Village, Hiccup and Fishlegs changed into dry(ish) clothes. (Berk was one of those damp places where clothes never really dried. They just became warm and wet rather than cold and wet.)

They hurried as quickly as they could towards the Great Hall.

By the time they got there, Stoick had called a Big Meeting of Everybody and the Great Hall was already packed to bursting with great Hairy Hooligans jostling each other for a good view of the coffin, which had been placed on a table in front of the fire.

Bit by bit Hiccup and Fishlegs managed to wriggle their way through the crowd to the front.

'Ah, Hiccup, there you are,' said Hiccup's father Stoick the Vast absent-mindedly, as he consulted with the other Elders in front of the coffin.

Stoick was a terrifying red-headed bull of a man whose belly turned a corner a good foot or two before the rest of him.

'Interesting find you've made here, my boy,' said Stoick, ruffling his son's hair proudly. 'The Lost Treasure of Grimbeard the Ghastly, eh?'

'Yes, Father, but...' said Hiccup.

'We're just about to open it,' said Stoick.

'But what *I'm* trying to say is,' interrupted Old Wrinkly (the cleverest and most ancient Elder of the Hooligan Tribe), 'it is written quite clearly on the top, "DO NOT OPEN THIS COFFIN, Cursed be he who disturbs the remains of Grimbeard the Ghastly, the greatest pirate who ever struck Terror into the Inner Isles"... In my considerable experience it is always a good idea NOT TO OPEN a coffin that says "DO NOT OPEN" on the front...'

'I agree,' said Hiccup nervously. 'Grimbeard the Ghastly was a nasty piece of work. Anybody who opens that coffin could be in for a horrible shock.'

'Rubbish,' scoffed Stoick the Vast. 'A warning like

Stoick the Vast thinking

NOW. What would a GREAT LEADER do in this situation?

that to put off grave-robbers should not stay
the hand of Fearsome Vikings like ourselves. Shall we,
who laugh in the face of Death and spit in the eye of
the Great Typhoon, quail at a simple curse to scare
infants and old men?'

Cries of 'No!' and 'Not likely, guv'nor!'

'All those in favour of opening up the box and
seeing whether the Lost Treasure of Grimbeard the
Ghastly is inside say AYE!'

'AYE!!!' bellowed out every member of the
Hooligan Tribe, except for Fishlegs, Old Wrinkly and
Hiccup.

'R-r-run for your lives!' yelped Toothless,
and hid in Hiccup's shirt. Fishlegs edged backwards
into the crowd.

'NOT a good idea, NOT a good idea,
NOT a good idea,' muttered Hiccup. He started
backing away from the coffin as Stoick fiddled
clumsily with the iron clasps.

'NOT a good idea, NOT a good idea, NOT A
GOOD IDEA,' repeated Hiccup as Stoick slowly
c-r-e-a-k-e-d up the coffin lid...

c-r-e-e-e-e-e-e-e-e-e-e-e-a-k...

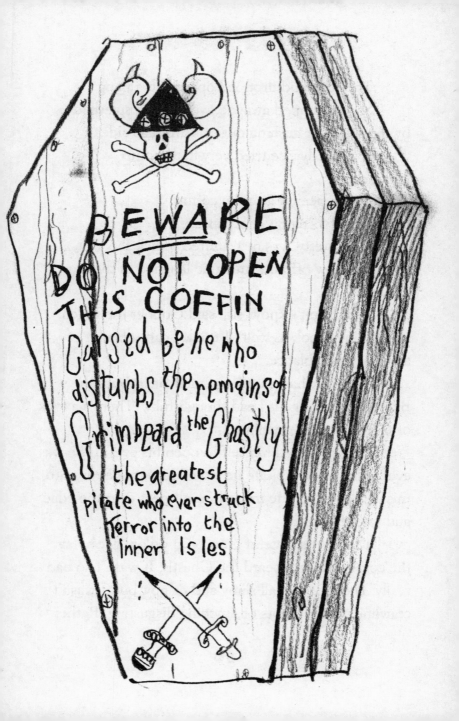

The coffin lid dropped open with a bang.

Stoick jumped away to avoid being splashed by the seawater gushing out of it from all sides.

Everybody else tried very hard not to look nervous.

Stoick peered into the coffin.

There was a bit of a pause.

'Not pretty, was he?' sniffed Stoick the Vast, trying to show off how much he laughed in the face of Death.

'Oh, I don't know, sir,' said Gobber the Belch, leaning in to look as well. 'I think I can see a bit of a family resemblance.'

'I know what you mean,' said Baggybum the Beerbelly, turning his head thoughtfully. 'There's a look of Great Aunt Heftythighs.'

Hiccup forced himself to open his eyes. If he was ever going to be a pirate he would have to get used to this sort of thing. He made himself peer over the edge and into the coffin.

There, in a state of green and yellow decay, lay the corpse of Grimbeard the Ghastly. It wasn't so bad really. The face was all slimy and drippy, but it wasn't crawling with maggots or anything disgusting. Rather peaceful really, lying so still…

And then Hiccup was sure he saw one of
the paper-white fingers twitch slightly.

He blinked and stared hard at it.

Nothing for a second.

And then… there it was again, a definite
quivering…

'The c-c-corpse!' stuttered Hiccup, 'it's
m-m-moving!'

'Nonsense, boy!' snapped Gobber the Belch.
'How can he possibly move? He's **DEAD**, isn't he?'
And he gave the corpse a prod with one fat forefinger.

The corpse of Grimbeard the Ghastly snapped
straight upright, propelled by some appalling force
from within it, yellow eyes popping, dribbly green face
contorted in a ghastly grimace.

'Aaaaaargh,' gurgled the corpse of Grimbeard the Ghastly, straight into the face of Gobber the Belch.

'AAAAAAAAAAAAAAAAAARGH!' screeched Gobber the Belch, jumping quite three feet in the air with his hair and his beard sticking out in all directions with the shock of it.

'AAAAAAAAAAAAAAAAAARGH!' yelled the rest of the Tribe.

For while Hooligans do indeed laugh in the face of Death and spit in the eye of the Great Typhoon, they have a morbid fear of the SUPERNATURAL.

Stoick dived underneath the table with his arms over his head in the vague belief that if he couldn't see IT, IT couldn't see HIM.

Seawater poured out of the coffin. The corpse of Grimbeard the Ghastly made disgusting choking noises. The veins on its popping yellow eyes stood out, its grey mouth quivered horribly.

Only Old Wrinkly remained calm.

'Don't panic,' said Old Wrinkly, 'this is NOT the corpse of Grimbeard the Ghastly...'

Hiccup had frozen in sheer terror. But he trusted Old Wrinkly, and he opened his eyes.

Nobody else took any notice whatsoever.

58

Gobber
the Belch
jumped quite
three feet
in the air
with the
shock of
it...

They went on panicking like crazy.

'Woden preserve me from the terminally stupid,' muttered Old Wrinkly under his breath, and he started yelling, as this was the only language the Hooligans really understood. 'DON'T PANIC! THIS IS NOT THE CORPSE OF GRIMBEARD THE GHASTLY!'

As he yelled he patted the corpse-that-wasn't-a-corpse hard on the back. Seawater spluttered out of it in all directions, gushing out of its nose and ears and mouth.

It wasn't the corpse of Grimbeard the Ghastly. Now that it had recovered from its coughing fit, it was clearly a tall, good-looking man, very much alive, if a little green from the effects of the sea water.

'So…' said Stoick, from under the table, 'that is DEFINITELY NOT the corpse of Grimbeard the Ghastly?'

The corpse-that-wasn't-a-corpse shook its head.

'Oh no,' it said faintly, 'definitely not. Easy mistake to make, but no, I'm not.'

And it slithered out of the coffin in a rush of seawater. It removed its helmet and, under the circumstances, performed a remarkably graceful bow.

'The name is Alvin. Alvin the... er...
Poor-But-Honest-Farmer.'

Alvin had quick, clever, laughing eyes.
He had a long, elegant moustache, a little limp from
the seawater. He smiled a charming, easy-going smile
(although a fussy person might think that perhaps it
had too many teeth in it).

Alvin stepped gracefully forward to pat Hiccup
on the head.

'And who might YOU be then, sonny?'

'Hiccup Horrendous Haddock the Third,'
stammered Hiccup.

'Greetings,' said Alvin the Poor-But-Honest-
Farmer.

He stooped to peer under the table. 'I presume
from your air of natural authority that you must be the
Chief of this Tribe?'

'Stoick the Vast,' replied Stoick.

Alvin clapped a hand to his forehead.

'Not THE Stoick the Vast, Terror of the Seas,
Most High Ruler of the Hooligans, O Hear His Name
and Tremble, Ugh, Ugh? By an EXTRAORDINARY
coincidence, you are the very man I have been
searching for.'

Stoick crawled out from under the table, staggered to his feet and puffed out his chest.

'That's me,' said Stoick the Vast, in much of his old hearty manner. 'And, may I ask, if you're *not* the corpse of Grimbeard the Ghastly, what in Woden's name were you doing in his coffin?'

'What a remarkably bright question,' replied Alvin enthusiastically, 'and if I could just sit down in this comfortable-looking chair? It's been a long day...'

'Of course, of course,' said Stoick, dusting off his throne.

'... I would be delighted to tell you my Tale...' said Alvin.

Toothless didn't like the look of Alvin...

6. THE TALE OF ALVIN THE POOR-BUT-HONEST-FARMER

The whole of the Tribe of Hairy Hooligans sat round-eyed, in silence, as Alvin settled himself into Stoick's throne and told his Tale.

'I was put in the coffin,' began Alvin, 'by some very rude people who not only disbelieved the Tale I am about to tell you but also suspected me of being a common thief. They dumped me over the side of the Harbour on their island with a lot of rude laughter...'

'Meatheads,' said Stoick knowledgeably. 'Were they led by a tall chap, one eye, bad breath, answers to the name of Mogadon?'

'That does ring a bell,' admitted Alvin.

'But how had you come across the coffin in the first place?' asked Stoick.

'I am a poor but honest farmer,' said Alvin, 'and a long time ago in the Peaceable Country, far far away, I was digging up some ground for... er... planting potatoes when I came across this coffin which... er... just fell open in my hands.'

'And when you opened this coffin which says

63

Alvin the
Poor-But-Honest-Farmer

quite clearly "DO NOT OPEN" on the front,' asked
Old Wrinkly thoughtfully, 'was there not some sort
of surprise?'

'You could say that,' admitted Alvin with a
good-natured smile that perhaps did not quite reach
his eyes. 'I opened the coffin, reached forward quite
innocently to grasp something inside… and the coffin
lid snapped shut with the force of a shark's jaws and in
one stroke cut off my hand.'

Alvin held up his right arm.

There, where his hand should have been
emerging from his sleeve, was an iron claw.

The Hooligans gasped in horror.

'Dearie me,' tutted Stoick. 'BOOBY-TRAPPED.
I do apologise for my great-grandfather. He did have
a nasty sense of humour.'

'Yeeesss,' said Alvin, smiling happily once more,
'but luckily us Poor-But-Honest-Farmers can take
a joke… And this,' he gestured to the claw, 'is very
handy for opening up oysters… Now, back to my
Tale. I was careful the next time I opened the coffin
to dismantle the booby trap first, but there was no
sign of any Treasure inside, nor indeed the body of
Grimbeard the Ghastly… What there *was*…'

The entire Tribe of Hairy Hooligans leaned forward eagerly, mouths open, eyes wide...

'... was *this* map*, and *this* riddle.'

Alvin reached into his breast pocket and held up the map and the riddle for everybody to see.

'Oh,' said Stoick, very disappointed. 'No Grimbeard? No treasure? No Stormblade? Just two little pieces of paper?'

'Ah, but Stoick,' said Alvin craftily, 'these two little pieces of paper will LEAD us to Grimbeard's treasure.'

'US?' said Old Wrinkly. 'Something is puzzling me. You have the riddle, you have the map, why didn't you just go and find the treasure yourself? Why did you come here to us?'

'But that would be dishonest!' said Alvin virtuously. 'We all know the Saga of "The Lost Treasure of Grimbeard the Ghastly"... This treasure belongs to you, his descendants. Besides, there's the little matter of the riddle. The riddle makes it clear that this treasure cannot be found by just *anybody*.'

Alvin cleared his throat.

---

*See page 10 for the Treasure Map of Grimbeard the Ghastly.

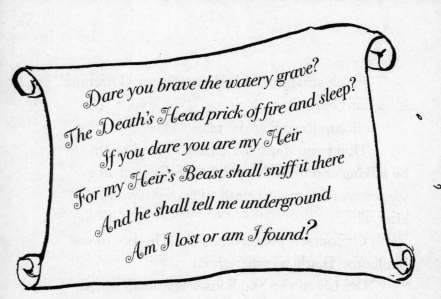

Dare you brave the watery grave?
The Death's Head prick of fire and sleep?
If you dare you are my Heir
For my Heir's Beast shall sniff it there
And he shall tell me underground
Am I lost or am I found?

'So you see,' said Alvin, 'it seems only the Heir
to Grimbeard the Ghastly can find the treasure…
And only his beast can sniff it out. I assume by 'Beast'
he means dragon.'

Dragons were excellent sniffers and finders
of Treasure. A good dragon could sniff out gold and
precious metals even when they were buried some
way below ground.

'And I couldn't possibly find this treasure
myself,' said Alvin, 'because I don't have a way with
dragons. They just DON'T LIKE ME, I don't know
what it is. Anyway, I wonder if any of you have any
idea of where the riddle is talking about? You, for
instance, Stoick, with your quick and lively brain?'

Stoick struggled to look intelligent. 'Hmmmm, it's a hard one...'

Hiccup looked at the map.

'Don't you think the Death's Head might be talking about the Isle of the Skullions, Father?' suggested Hiccup. 'A Death's Head is a skull, after all...'

'Of course!' boomed Stoick. 'The Isle of the Skullions! That'll be where it is!'

The Isle of the Skullions was a small island off the west coast of Berk that formed the shape of a skull-and-crossbones. It was this shape that Grimbeard had adopted for his flag and, most famously, his helmet.

'So this island here is the Isle of the Skullions, is it?' purred Alvin gleefully, pointing at the map. 'And that's where we'll find our treasure?'

To Alvin's surprise the Hooligans started laughing.

'Oh, there's no question of finding the treasure if it's on the Isle of the Skullions,' said Stoick cheerfully. 'Nobody has *ever* returned from the Isle of the Skullions ALIVE. Hiccup, you're the expert on dragons, you explain to Alvin about Skullions...'

The SKULLION

The Skullion is a dragon standing about 10 feet tall. It has lost the power of flight, eyesight and hearing but its sense of smell is phenomenal and it will eat anythign it comes across. This animal is untrainable and very, very dangerous

---

~STATISTICS~

COLOURS: Black and purple
ARMED WITH: Terrifying teeth, claws etc.
FEAR FACTOR:..............9
ATTACK:.......................9
SPEED:...........................9
SIZE:...............................7
DISOBEDIENCE:.................9

'The Skullion,' said Hiccup, always delighted to be asked a natural history question, 'is a very rare, very savage species of flightless dragon. Despite being blind and very nearly deaf, it is one of the most fearsome predators of all dragons, hunting in packs using a highly developed sense of smell alone...'

'OK, OK,' said Stoick hurriedly, 'we get the picture...'

'It has this one extra-long super-sharp claw,' continued Hiccup, 'with which it disables its victims by cutting the Achilles tendon at the back of their heels, leaving them unable to walk. It then eats them alive.'

NOT very nice.

'Ahhhhh,' said Alvin. 'I see the problem. But I am sure a man as clever as you, Stoick, will be able to lead a quest to the Isle of the Skullions to find this treasure nonetheless.'

'A quest to the Isle of the Skullions would be total madness,' said Old Wrinkly firmly.

'Grimbeard's sword, the Stormblade, will be part of this treasure,' wheedled Alvin. 'And if you held the Stormblade the name of Hooligan would be feared again throughout the barbarian world...'

70

Stoick stroked his beard thoughtfully.

'And you, Stoick,' cooed Alvin, 'picture your-self with diamonds sprinkled in your beard, a golden breastplate, the Stormblade flaming terribly in one hand, bracelets for those handsome wrists of yours. I can see you already, Mogadon kneeling humbly before you. What a vision you will be!'

Stoick sucked in his belly and flexed his muscles. He'd always secretly fancied himself in a pair of earrings.

'I'LL DO IT!' he yelled.

'FELLOW HOOLIGANS!' he bellowed. 'I shall lead you on a quest to find the treasure of our ancestors!'

'But it's insane!' cried Hiccup. 'Anyone who sets one toe on that island will be eaten alive in moments! It's suicide to even think of it!'

Everyone was cheering too hard to listen to Hiccup.

'Glory and riches shall be ours,' beamed Stoick, patting Alvin painfully hard on the back.

'Oh, here we gooo...' moaned Hiccup to himself.

7. PRACTISING SWORDFIGHTING AND SNIFFING FOR TREASURE

In Hiccup's opinion, everything went wrong from the moment Alvin the Poor-But-Honest-Farmer was let out of the coffin. It wasn't Alvin's fault, of course. He was a most entertaining and enjoyable companion.

He made the women blush by praising their muscles and their fat yellow plaits. He made the men laugh with hilarious farty jokes and impressions of Mogadon the Meathead. He made the children adore him by telling stories of the trickeries and battles of long-dead Heroes.

Hiccup liked him, too.

Alvin came across Hiccup one day, practising his swordfighting for the second depressing hour in a row.

Hiccup was trying to do the 'Grimbeard's Grapple', and failing miserably every time. Stoick had given him a new sword to replace the Scaremaker, an impressively large and heavy one called a Stretchapoint.

'Got a lot of LENGTH to it, my boy,' Stoick had

said. 'It'll make up for your shortness of arm. Give you a better reach.'

But Hiccup had difficulty keeping it steady, and when he got to the lunge at the end he tended to fall over. He had just got up and wearily picked up the Stretchapoint for another go, when Alvin the Poor-But-Honest-Farmer suddenly appeared right behind him and said, 'Hiccup, isn't it?'

Hiccup was so startled he nearly fell over again. He hadn't realised he was being watched.

'You're the Heir to Stoick the Vast, aren't you?' smiled Alvin.

Hiccup sighed. 'Well, I hope so,' he said. 'That's the general idea, anyway. But unless I get better at this swordfighting, I'm never going to be anybody's Heir.

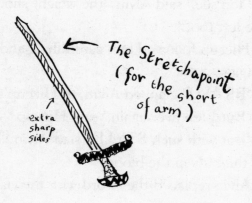

The Stretchapoint
(for the short of arm)

extra sharp sides

I'm HOPELESS at it.'

'No, no,' said Alvin reassuringly, 'you've got natural ability, I can see that. You just need a little coaching, that's all. Let me show you.'

Alvin carefully put his helmet by the side of the ferns for safekeeping. Hiccup watched, fascinated, as he untwisted the claw attached to his right arm. In its place he fixed a 'sword-holder' mechanism. He then drew his sword and showed Hiccup how he could fit it into the mechanism. He twisted it tight so it wouldn't fall off.

'A clever little contraption I designed myself,' said Alvin. 'I think I fight even better now than I did before the accident...' He twirled his moustache and demonstrated the Grapple himself.

'You see,' said Alvin, 'the weight should be kept on the left foot.'

Hiccup followed him carefully... and fell over again.

'BRAVO!' clapped Alvin, to Hiccup's surprise.

'But I fell over again,' said Hiccup.

'But with such STYLE,' said Alvin. 'You can't teach that, it's in the blood.'

Alvin replaced the sword with the claw and

picked up his helmet. He made a grimace as he put it back on his head. He took it off again and peered inside. 'There seems to be some sort of MUD in here, some sort of very SMELLY mud...'

'It's all over your hair, I'm afraid, sir,' said Hiccup.

Alvin looked horrified. He was very particular about his personal appearance. He hurried away to wash it off.

Toothless, who had been hunting rats through the ferns, came and perched on Hiccup's shoulder. He had the giggles.

Eventually, when he got his breath back, he choked out, 'P-p-pooed in his helmet...'

'TOOTHLESS!' scolded Hiccup. 'That's revolting and unkind. Why did you poo in poor Alvin's helmet?'

'H-h-he's a BAD MAN,' replied Toothless.

'Who, Alvin the Poor-But-Honest-Farmer?' asked Hiccup in surprise. 'Don't be so prejudiced, Toothless, just because he's not from round these parts doesn't make him a bad man...'

'S-s-suit yourself,' shrugged Toothless, checking out his wings for dragonfleas. 'Toothless thinks he's an O-O-Outcast.'

Hiccup started nervously.

Outcasts were Vikings who were so vicious, so terrible and sneaking and burglarous, that they had been cast out of regular Viking society, and had formed an extraordinarily ferocious Tribe of their own. It was even rumoured that some Outcasts ate their enemies.

'Oh, come ON,' protested Hiccup. 'He doesn't

Toothless doing a poo in Alvin's helmet

look anything LIKE an Outcast.'

'Y-y-you ever seen one?' asked Toothless.

'Well, no,' admitted Hiccup, 'but neither have you, and you haven't a shred of evidence. Let's go and get some lunch and forget this rubbish.'

That conversation sowed a little seed of doubt in Hiccup's mind.

He was already feeling uneasy because he knew that he and all the other boys were going to have to join in this suicidal quest to the Isle of the Skullions, which would set out just as soon as Stoick and Alvin had worked out a Plan to avoid the Tiny Problem of everybody being eaten alive the moment they landed on the island.

And he knew that he, Hiccup, as the Heir to

the Hairy Hooligans, was supposed to be the one
to find the treasure. So when he wasn't doing his
swordfighting, or being shouted at by Gobber on
the Training Programme, he was bustling Toothless
out of the door to practise sniffing for treasure.

The first morning was typical. Fishlegs turned
up with his dragon Horrorcow, and they stood
watching in polite astonishment as Hiccup went
through the elaborate game of getting Toothless out
of the front door.

Firstly, Hiccup went through the house shouting
Toothless's name.

No answer.

Next, Hiccup stole a mackerel from the larder.

'Ohhhhh, Toothless,' he sang craftily, waving
the fishy stench around a bit to get Toothless's
interest. 'I've got a lovely piece of mackerel for you.'

A very muffled but thoughtful voice replied,
'T-t-toothless sick. T-t-toothless can't come out
'cos he's V-V-VERY VERY sick.'

'Then you won't want this mackerel then,' sang
Hiccup.

Another pause.

'M-m-mackerel good for the sick. Have

mackerel but NO GO OUT.'

Hiccup had worked out where the voice was coming from. He peered up the chimney, and there was Toothless, hanging upside-down in a cloud of smoke.

'NO, Toothless,' said Hiccup in his firmest voice. 'You have the mackerel, you have to go out, THAT'S the deal. And you have to PROMISE.'

'OK, then,' said Toothless, flapping out of the chimney, 'Toothless p-p-promise.'

Hiccup held out the mackerel.

With a shriek of 'T-T-TOOTHLESS CROSSED HIS CLAWS!' Toothless grabbed the fish, pushed Hiccup heavily in the chest, and disappeared at high speed into the other room, leaving Hiccup to topple over into the fireplace in a cloud of ash.

It didn't take long for Hiccup to find him again.

A tell-tale drift of bluey-grey smoke was curling out from the end of Stoick's bed.

Hiccup tiptoed up and dragged him out from under the bedclothes.

With a squawk of outrage, Toothless grabbed hold of one of the bedknobs in his powerful jaws.

Hiccup got him by the tail and pulled.

79

LEARNING TO SPEAK DRAGONESE

Dragonese is punctuated by shrill shrieks
and popping noises, and sounds
MOST EXTRAORDINARY
when spoken by a human. The word
'pishyou', for example, is pronounced
very like a sneeze.

MORE COMMON DRAGON PHRASES:

Pishyou na munch-munch di miaow-miaow
Please do not eat the cat

≈

Hoody chuck-it-up un di jim-jams di pappa?
Who has been sick in my father's pyjamas?

≈

PARKA DI BOTTY, forsakes di Woden,
or me do di girly boo-hoo.
SIT, for Woden's sake, before I burst into tears

≈

(To big dragons): Mi wobblediguts bigtime.
I am very poisonous

≈

'Come ON, Toothless,' said Hiccup, 'time for sniffing practice...' He tickled Toothless under one wing. Toothless wriggled a bit, going red in the face. Hiccup tickled him under the other.

Toothless let go, giggling, and there was a short kerfuffle, in which Toothless bit Hiccup several times, before Hiccup finally got him under control, tucking him under one arm and holding his mouth shut with the other.

'Now,' said Hiccup, 'you know we have to practise the sniffing. You want us to find the treasure, don't you, not Fireworm or Seaslug? You want us to show everybody what amazing sniffers Toothless Daydreams really are, don't you?'

Toothless nodded, still with Hiccup holding his mouth shut.

'Well then,' said Hiccup, 'we have to practise. Promise you won't bite me any more, and no claw-crossing?'

As soon as Hiccup had removed his fingers Toothless went all limp and floppy.

'T-t-toothless so w-w-weak... can't sniff when he's so w-w-weak...' he moaned pathetically.

'RIGHT,' said Hiccup, 'you can have the

81

other half of the mackerel if you BEHAVE FROM NOW ON.'

'OK, then,' grumbled Toothless, shaking his wings. 'T-t-toothless Daydreams such g-g-g-good sniffers they don't have to p-p-practise, but OK.'

Hiccup and Fishlegs scraped the disgusting mess of the rest of the mackerel from the bottom of Stoick's bed – Stoick was NOT going to be pleased – and fed it to Toothless, as well as a small haddock pie and three or four oysters.

'He won't be able to FLY at this rate,' said Fishlegs.

They set off into the hills and bogs of Berk, Toothless whining the whole way, 'C-c-carry me, c-c-carry me, my w-w-wings ache... Are we n-n-nearly there yet?'

Berk was always a wild looking place, tree-less and boggy, heather-blown and fern-filled. And, of course, it was practically always raining, anything from a light, persistent drizzle to a drenching downpour. (There are twenty-eight words that mean 'rain' in the Hooligan language.)

But if you like your landscapes bleak and dramatic, Berk was attractive in its own way, and this was now spoilt by the great muddy holes the Hooligans were digging everywhere, ever since they had become obsessed with hunting for treasure.

What with avoiding the holes, and wading through waist-high gorse and bracken, it took the boys an hour or so even to get up into the hills to practise. And by the time they got there, Horrorcow had fallen into such a deep sleep on Fishlegs's shoulder it was impossible to wake her.

Hiccup brought out an old gold bracelet of his mother's for Toothless to sniff.

'That's the smell you're looking for,' he said.

'N-n-no problem,' said Toothless. 'Easy-p-p-peasy...'

After two hot and breathless hours of running around after Toothless and digging where he said he could sniff something, the boys surveyed what they had found.

1 turnip
3 rabbits (couldn't catch them)
1 small broken spoon

Um... that's it, really.

Hiccup shook his head mournfully. 'It's not good, is it?'

'Not good? NOT GOOD??' exclaimed a jeering voice behind them. 'It's *pathetic*, that's what it is.'

Hiccup turned round, and there was Snotlout, laughing so hard Dogsbreath had to hold him upright.

'I mean, a VEGETABLE and a PIECE OF CUTLERY?' Snotlout wiped the tears from his eyes. 'It's just so brilliantly Useless...'

'Do you really think,' tittered Snotlout, once he had recovered somewhat, '*that* microscopic amoeba,' Snotlout pointed at Toothless, 'is going to

84

lead you to TREASURE? He couldn't sniff his
way to his own bottom.'

Toothless bristled angrily.

'But then he's just a mongrel Common or
Garden...' scoffed Snotlout.

'Toothless-not-repeat-not-a-Common-or-
Garden-D-d-dragon!' howled Toothless. 'Toothless
VERY RARE breed c-c-called a Toothless
Daydream...'

'Now, Fireworm here is a Monstrous Nightmare,
one of your pure hunting greenbloods... Look what
a REAL hunting dragon can find if she puts her nose
to it...' Snotlout reached into a bag slung round his
waist and drew out a large silver plate, a dagger with
ancient runes winding round the handle and a couple
of pretty bead necklaces.

'And that's only an afternoon's work,' said
Snotlout.

Fireworm purred with pleasure.
She shrugged her beautiful, shining,
blood-red shoulders.

'To the nose of an aristocrat
like myself,' she hissed, 'the thing was
reeking like a week-old haddock.'

85

'Naturally,' said Toothless, 'if you have a nose the s-s-size of an elephant seal it m-m-makes life easy for you.'

Fireworm's nostrils flared furiously. 'I have a beautifully proportioned nose,' she snapped.

'Now, now, Fireworm,' chided Snotlout, who didn't understand Dragonese but knew they were trading insults, 'don't let the peasants upset you. Just think of when we get to the Isle of the Skullions and you sniff out the treasure and everybody will know that *I* am the true heir to the Hairy Hooligans...
Nice thought, isn't it, Useless?'

Snotlout leant forward, and with the edge of the plate he was holding, pushed Hiccup ve-ry gently backwards until he overbalanced into the mud.

'Har Har Har Har Har!' snorted Snotlout and Dogsbreath, and they sauntered off.

It was very depressing.

All in all, ever since Alvin arrived, Hiccup had been walking around with a sick feeling in his stomach and a prickle of fear crawling spiderishly down the back of his neck.

It wasn't just the thought of the quest to the Isle of the Skullions (although he was already having

86

nightmares about being ripped to pieces by pan-ther-like creatures with teeth like broken glass). It was this feeling that there was something evil, something POISONOUS lurking on the Isle of Berk.

And that something really terrible was going to happen... sometime soon...

Does this look like the sort of dragon who would poo in a helmet?

8. MEANWHILE, IN A CAVERN DEEP, DEEP UNDERGROUND

Meanwhile, in a Cavern deep, deep underground, a small Deadly Nadder was crying for its mother.

It had wandered away from its home in the cosy tunnels of the Dragon Nursery, and lost itself in the maze of the Caliban Caves below.

Gradually, as it flapped frantically down wrong turning after wrong turning, the happy hissings and squawkings of its fellow dragons had grown fainter and fainter. For the last hour it had heard only the unhappy echoes of itself as it crept deeper and deeper into the blackness.

What is more, it had the bad luck to stumble into a Cavern inhabited by a gigantic creature who was guarding something precious. This was a far larger and scarier killing-machine than a mere Skullion. It was at least a hundred years old, and living for a century in such gloomy depths had done very little for its soul or its brain. It was lonely and bitter, and had a longing for the light, which it had never seen. But most of all it was permanently hungry.

The little Nadder cried for its mother again, and hopped a bit farther forward.

A singularly unattractive sludgy tentacle curled its way around the small dragon and lifted it into the air.

The Creature did something to the Nadder to kill it, something most unpleasant, and the poor little animal let out a last shriek of absolute terror...

And then all was silence.

PIRATE TRAINING PROGRAMME TIMETABLE

Name: Hiccup H.H. III

	MONDAY	TUESDAY	WEDNESDAY	THURSDAY	FRIDAY
	SWORDFIGHTING AT SEA	*Don't forget gumboots!* SHOUTING	FRIGHTENING FOREIGNERS	ROBBERY	BASIC BURGLARY
	SWORDFIGHTING AT SEA	DRAGON TRAINING	FRIGHTENING FOREIGNERS	SENSELESS VIOLENCE	BASIC BURGLARY
	[break]	[break]	[break]	[break]	[break]
	SPITTING	ADVANCED RUDERY	WEAPONRY	ADVANCED RUDERY *My favourite.* NOT	BADD SPPELING
	[break] Fishlegs Gobber	BASHYBALL *Yuck*	[break]	[break]	[break]
	BASIC BURGLARY	BASHYBALL *Yuck*	DRAGON TRAINING	POINTLESS GRAFFITI	SENSELESS VIOLENCE
	FRIGHTENING FOREIGNERS		DRAGON TRAINING	POINTLESS GRAFFITI *art lesson*	SENSELESS VIOLENCE
	SPITTING	ADVANCED RUDERY	WEAPONRY	SENSELESS VIOLENCE	BADD SPPELING HOOMWURK

Homework: SPITTING

9. THE ADVANCED RUDERY LESSON IS INTERRUPTED

This jumpy time of waiting and preparing finally came to an end about two weeks later.

It was halfway through one of Gobber's Advanced Rudery lessons in the Great Hall.

Snotlout was in front of the rest of the class, having a Rudery Battle against Tuffnut Junior. Tuffnut Junior was struggling. He was naturally a good-natured boy, and insults were not his strong point.

'You,' said Tuffnut Junior, trying to sound sneery, 'are a big fat... and I mean really, *really* fat... BULLY... and your granny is a... your granny is a... your granny is a... very naughty person...'

'Oh, for Thor's sake, Tuffnut Junior!' exploded Gobber furiously, tearing his beard out. 'This is a *simple* exercise, can't you do better than THAT? Snotlout's granny is a yellow-bellied decrepit old oyster, Snotlout's granny is a barking mad old walrus-head...'

'Wossat????' howled Snotlout, so psyched up for the lesson that he didn't care *who* he attacked.

'No, no,
Snotlout,' soothed
Gobber, 'not *really*, I'm
just telling Tuffnut... you're
supposed to think of something
EXTRA VILE and then spit the words
out... you show him Snotlout.'

'With pleasure,' leered Snotlout. He leaned
forward until his nose was just inches away from
Tuffnut's. He grabbed Tuffnut around the neck for
extra emphasis. His mean little eyes narrowed with
menace, his nostrils quivered with temper.

'*You*,' he spat out with savage contempt, 'are a
cowardly cowering cuttlefish...'

'BRILLIANT, Snotlout, BRILLIANT,' cheered
Gobber.

'... with the heart of a jellyfish, the brains of

a plankton, and the stink of a barrelful of mackerel-heads.'

'Oh BRAVO,' boomed Gobber, 'you go straight to the top of the class. At this rate, Snotlout, you will have no problems whatsoever becoming a pirate, which is more than I can say for the rest of you...'

ETC, ETC, ETC...

Hiccup raised his eyes to the heavens. He went on absent-mindedly drawing pictures in his Insults Book.

He was unexpectedly interrupted by the arrival of Stoick the Vast, and behind him, smiling charmingly, Alvin the Poor-But-Honest-Farmer.

'I apologise for disturbing your lesson, Gobber,' beamed Stoick.

'Not at all, not at all,' said Gobber.

'But I bring GOOD NEWS. We are about to set out on our glorious QUEST TO THE ISLE OF THE SKULLIONS!!'

There was a short silence, in which Fishlegs turned white as a sheet and made faint moaning noises.

And then everybody else started cheering.

Hiccup put up his hand.

ME

Snotlout

help

Name __Hiccup H·H· III__

Subject __Insults Book__

__Advanced Rudeny__

Form _____

Gobber is a girly

I HEERD that · NO YOU DO

wate till I gett yoo ↓

Dogsbreath has a face like a squashed oyster

If lost please return to:
Hiccup H. Haddock III
Isle of Berk
The Icy Wastes
Northern Barbaria
Planet Earth   Toothless
The Universe   Endless Spa

94

'What about the Skullions?' he asked.

'I'm glad you asked that,' replied Stoick the Vast enthusiastically. 'As we all know,' he patted Hiccup affectionately on the head, 'Skullions are terrifyingly vicious creatures...'

'Savage beyond your wildest dreams,' murmured Hiccup.

'BUT,' beamed Stoick, 'they have not only lost their ability to fly, but also their sense of SIGHT. Indeed, they are guided to their prey almost entirely by smell alone. So it is Alvin's theory that if we BATH thoroughly before we go – unusual, I know, but you have to suffer to be rich – we should be all right.'

Fishlegs put up his hand. 'Theory? *Should* be? What you're saying is that Alvin doesn't actually KNOW, and we could find ourselves flat on our backs being chewed to death very slowly by a bunch of ravenous reptiles.'

Stoick nodded.

'In which case you shall enter Vallhalla a Hero of the Tribe! And may I say here,' said Stoick solemnly, 'that anyone who dies in the course of his duty shall be awarded a posthumous Black Helmet.'

'Oh yippee,' murmured Hiccup.

'DEATH OR GLORY!' yelled Stoick the Vast, performing the complicated Hooligan salute, which consists of making a slitting motion across your own throat while letting out a fart like a clap of thunder.

'DEATH OR GLORY!' shouted Gobber the Belch, and eleven of the trainees shouted fanatically, 'DEATH OR GLORY!' and made the salute back at him.

'OH, not this AGAIN,' groaned Hiccup and Fishlegs to themselves.

Stoick and Alvin's plan really was that simple. The Hooligans and dragons had to bath themselves thoroughly. They had to present themselves the next day at the Great Hall, where Alvin would make sure they passed what Alvin called 'the Sniff Test'. This consisted of Alvin, who was good at this sort of thing, seeing if he could smell them or not, and the expedition would set off.

Hiccup nerved himself up to talk to his father, never an easy task.

'Father,' said Hiccup to Stoick, after he had bathed himself and Toothless very thoroughly indeed.

'Hmmmm?' replied Stoick absent-mindedly. He was attempting to dry off his own dragon,

OH, not tHis AGAIN..?

Newtsbreath, in front of the fire.

Newtsbreath was an acne-covered sludge green
Gronckle the size of a small lion. He loathed water.
It had taken Stoick forty minutes to catch him and
dump him in the tub. Now he made a furious lunge at
Stoick, grabbing his left forearm between his massive
jaws. Stoick laughed merrily and gave him a sharp
whack on the nose with the scrubbing brush.

'Now, now, Newtsbreath,' chided Stoick,
'don't be grumpy.'

'I'm worried,' continued Hiccup, 'that we may
be setting out on the wrong quest. Do you really think
we should be looking for treasure? We're quite happy
and peaceful enough without all that money.'

Stoick ruffled Hiccup's hair affectionately.

'Don't you see,' said Stoick excitedly, 'YOU'RE going to be the one to find this treasure. That's what the riddle said, "Only the True Heir can find it." It has troubled me for some time that Baggybum and Snotlout might have their eyes on your throne. When YOU find the treasure, it will silence them forever. I'm doing this as much for YOU as for the gold and the glory, although I do see myself in a pair of fancy earrings, I must admit...'

'But what if I DON'T find the treasure?' asked Hiccup.

But Stoick wasn't listening. He had stomped off to get ready.

'Oh, bother,' said Hiccup.

Newtsbreath
in the bath

10. THE WORST DAY OF HICCUP'S LIFE SO FAR

At dawn on the day of the Quest, Hiccup got dressed very reluctantly indeed. He buckled on the sword his father had given him, hoping that it wouldn't get in the way too much. He slung a spade in a sling across his back, where he normally might have carried a bow-and-arrow. He was so nervous he couldn't eat his porridge.

He finally managed to drag Toothless out of bed and set off towards Hooligan Harbour, where everybody was meeting.

Toothless sat on his shoulder, angrily rubbing sleep out of his eyes with one wing.

'Toothless don't W-W-WANT to go on Quest,' he complained. 'Is s-s-stupid. Is s-s-silly. Is d-d-dangerous.'

Hiccup could not have agreed with him more, but all he said was, 'You're going to be all right. YOU'VE got wings. Any Skullions attack you, and you just fly away.'

'Yes, but T-t-t-toothless don't like the sight of b-b-blood...' whined Toothless. 'You get torn to pieces

99

and Toothless feel s-s-sick...'

'We all have our problems,' snapped Hiccup crossly.

Fishlegs was already at the Harbour, looking furious. His dragon, Horrorcow, sat at his feet, chewing quietly.

All the other boys were milling about, their dragons fighting each other or flapping over their heads. Everybody was thoroughly over-excited despite the very real prospect of being eaten alive.

DRAGON ARMOUR

head goes in here →

A cape made out of thick, heavy leather to protect the shoulders and chest.

100

'Who do you reckon would win if a Skullion was to fight a Bloody Crocoraptor in one-to-one combat?' chatted Wartihog.

'Oh, the Skullion would win EVERY TIME,' replied Clueless. 'No question. My father says the Skullion is one of the most vicious creatures on the planet. It'd just whip out that famous extra-long claw and swipe… it'd be Goodnight Crocoraptor…'

DRAGON GLOVE

Worn to protect the hand and upper arm while Dragon training

'Ah,' said Wartihog craftily, 'but what if the Skullion had one paw tied behind its back, who would win then?'

'Idiots,' fumed Fishlegs. 'Idiots!! I'm surrounded by people with seaweed for brains.'

Other than the boys, there were about fifty adult pirates in the Skullion landing party, all of Stoick's biggest and finest Warriors. Alvin was cracking jokes, giving out hearty handshakes and patting everybody on the back.

Stoick the Vast was delighted to be setting off on a military operation and marched about yelling orders.

'RIGHT, everybody. Once we've landed we split up into groups of two. We fan out across the island, and we get our dragons to sniff for the treasure. Notice you have all been supplied with a whistle – Gobber, could you demonstrate?'

Gobber blew a sharp blast on the whistle.

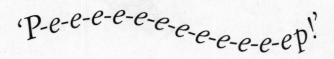

'Once you hear that noise you will realise that somebody has found the treasure. Make your way towards the sound as quickly as possible so we can all help to carry it back to the ship. REMEMBER, the dragons will be sleeping during the day and it does not matter how much noise you make because the Skullion is stone deaf. However, do try not to step on one and don't forget that their sense of smell is very acute indeed. So once you land on the island, **THERE WILL BE ABSOLUTELY NO FARTING WHATSOEVER.** Is that understood?'

The Warriors nodded solemnly.

'Righto, then,' said Stoick. 'Death or Glory.'

'DEATH OR GLORY!' yelled everybody.

And the Grimbeard's Treasure-Seeking Skullion Landing Party climbed aboard the good ship *Lucky Thirteen* to set sail for the Isle of the Skullions.

Dogsbreath the Duhbrain 'accidentally' bumped into Hiccup as they climbed in and knocked him on to the floor of the boat, where Snotlout trod on him.

'Clumsy me,' grinned Snotlout, swinging the Flashcut in a nonchalant fashion. 'Good luck, Useless.'

Lucky Thirteen set off slowly from the harbour through an ominous thick fog hanging heavily over the whole of the Inner Isles. It was difficult to see more than six feet ahead.

After three or four hours they caught sight of the Isle of the Skullions looming spookily through the mist. And Hiccup's immediate thoughts were, in no particular order, 'Let's go home! Turn around! ABANDON SHIP!'

'Don't sweat,' he told himself. 'Skullions can smell sweat.' But he could feel himself getting hotter and hotter with seasickness and fright as the island drew closer and closer...

In fact, even the bravest and most chatty of the Hooligans fell silent as they sailed deeper and deeper into waters their Tribe had been forbidden to enter for hundreds and hundreds of years.

For the Isle of the Skullions was a very sinister place.

The black cliffs in their odd pillar-like formations and the bloody bright-red earth seemed to whisper the word, 'Death.'

All around there were crazy towers of limpet shells stacked up in piles perilously high, like so many fantastic sculptures. Being unable to fly or swim, the Skullions were imprisoned on the island. They had long ago finished off any small mammals, reptiles or birds that had once lived there. For years they had had

to exist on shellfish, the limpet in particular because
it was so plentiful.

There was no sign of life anywhere. No rabbits,
mice or other scuttly creatures running around the
hillsides. No birds calling from the clifftops. Nor were
there any signs of the Skullions, either. There *were*,
however, worryingly enormous holes dotted all over the
landscape.

Those must be their burrows, thought Hiccup.

They were larger than any burrows Hiccup had
ever seen before. Some of the holes were as big as the
front door of the Great Hall.

They must be somewhere down there, thought Hiccup, swallowing hard.

Because there were no animals or birds, and no winds on such a calm day, there was an eerie silence.

Except, that is, for one, terrifying sound.

Imagine the set-your-teeth-on-edge screech of a chalk scratching on a blackboard multiplied hundreds of times over. It was the sort of noise you might get if you were sharpening a thousand knives on a thousand stones, but it was far more excruciating than that. It sent all of Hiccup's nerve-ends wincing and jangling, even as he realised what the horrible rhythmic scritch-scratch was.

It was the sound of the Skullions sharpening that extra-long claw of theirs on a rock deep within their burrows. This was a practice Hiccup knew about, but had never actually heard in real life before, called 'sleep-sharpening'.

Hiccup took a deep breath. *Well, at least we know they're asleep,* he thought.

The Hooligans had to row three-quarters of the way around the island before they found a place where the boats could land safely. It was a wide, open bay, again with that strange blood-red sand.

Alvin stood up to make a speech.

Every dragon on the boat hissed and growled warningly as he spoke.

'I wanted to wish everybody the best of Viking luck,' he said, smiling smoothly and easily. 'To my great, great sadness, I will not be able to join you on this part of the Quest. Nothing would give me greater pleasure than to risk my life in this glorious enterprise. But even though I have washed thoroughly I am afraid my smell is so strong to dragons that it might put the whole operation in jeopardy. I shall just stay here and look after the boats.'

'And it was all h-h-his idea in the first place!' said Toothless, outraged, in Hiccup's ear. 'S-see what Toothless means? An Outcast AND a c-c-coward...'

Stoick patted his friend sympathetically on the back. 'Very noble of you, Alvin,' he whispered loudly. (It was difficult not to whisper even though the creatures had no ears to hear with.) 'I'm sorry you have to miss out on the fun. OK, men, find yourself a partner, fan out across the island and if nobody finds anything at all, we'll meet back here in an hour.'

Fireworm was in a frenzy of excitement as soon as they landed. She had clearly scented something already, and was dying to follow it up, her tail thrashing, whimpering and dribbling with her eagerness to be off.

'Now, no following US,' grinned Snotlout, aiming a kick at Hiccup as he and Dogsbreath hurried after her.

Hiccup and Fishlegs stood looking at Toothless, but Toothless was showing no such joy at the task ahead. He sat calmly on the sand licking his tail in a thoughtful fashion. Fishlegs's dragon, Horrorcow, had already fallen asleep under a bench on the boat, so SHE was going to be no help.

'Can you sniff anything?' whispered Hiccup hopefully.

Toothless sniffed.

'POOH,' he said in disgust. 'Lergified limpets and s-s-sunbaked Skullions... Y-Y-Y-Y-YUCKY. L-l-l-l-let's get out of here.'

'No, no, no,' whispered Hiccup. 'Treasure. Gold. Jewels. That sort of thing.'

And he added craftily, 'I'm sure a TOOTHLESS DAYDREAM like yourself can sniff far better than a mere Monstrous Nightmare.'

Toothless swelled with indignation as he

remembered the cheek of that Fireworm creature. He sniffed some more.

'Toothless HAS got a slight c-c-c-cold,' he said with dignity, 'but that doesn't b-b-bother us aristocrats. There M-M-MIGHT be something coming from over there.'

And he waved a claw vaguely towards the left.

So Hiccup drew his too-big sword, and they set off, keeping a sharp eye out for any Skullions that might be awake.

They waded through waist-high ferns and endless heather, much as they might have done on Berk. At one point they passed a GIGANTIC footprint in the mud. Hiccup knelt down to examine it.

'Woden preserve us,' he murmured. 'This means the Skullion is about TWICE as big as we previously thought.'

'No question that it'd beat the Bloody Crocoraptor in one-to-one combat, then,' said Fishlegs, unable to stop himself from laughing hysterically. 'Oh, this is great, on top of everything else, I'm going CRAZY.'

Hiccup was feeling nervous about so many things it was difficult to concentrate on which worry to worry about most. He HAD to find the treasure. It was bad enough being the worst swordfighting trainee EVER, but if he didn't find this treasure that the Heir was supposed to find, then his father was going to be really disappointed. Hiccup hated disappointing his father, even though he had lots of practice at it.

And what if SNOTLOUT found the Treasure? Hiccup went cold and clammy at the thought.

He looked doubtfully at Toothless, who was hitching a ride perched on Fishlegs's spade. He had shown no promise whatsoever when they had been practising on Berk.

But Toothless had triumphed in a crisis before. When Hiccup was swallowed by a Seadragonus Giganticus Maximus, Toothless had flown up the Monster's nostril, causing him to sneeze, and saving Hiccup's life. So he DID have hidden and surprising depths.

Maybe he was a hidden Sniffer as well as a hidden Hero. Maybe he really HAD caught a whiff of something... Maybe...

Toothless thoughtfully picked his nose, examined the bogey on the end of one talon, and swallowed it. He suddenly flapped off the spade and started leading the little procession, in a worryingly aimless fashion. At one point he led them in a pointless circle. At another Hiccup stopped him in the nick of time before he woke up all the Skullions by doing a poo. Finally he settled on a small grassy patch at the top of a little hill. He sat down and scratched his ear.

'C-c-could be here,' he said absent-mindedly.

Hiccup's heart beat a little quicker.

'Here?' he asked. Toothless nodded in an offhand way. The boys took out their spades and, forgetting about the Skullions in their excitement, started to dig.

After about ten minutes of shovelling, they hit on an underground cache of limpet shells.

'Frittering Freya,' said Fishlegs. 'These Skullions eat a LOT of limpets. I bet this whole HILL is made out of limpets. I bet this whole ISLAND is made out of limpets...'

Hiccup's spade hit on something hard and large and heavy just below the surface. Hiccup held his breath. He prodded again. Yes, it was definitely hard and heavy.

'I think I've got something here,' he whispered.

Toothless leapt up and down in excitement.

'T-T-TREASURE! T-T-TREASURE!' he chanted. 'You going to be a Hero! And T-t-toothless the Hero's Dragon! You going to be...'

Hiccup reached down, caught an edge of the hard object and, struggling with both hands, p-u-l-l-e-d out of the earth...

The most gigantic limpet shell anyone had ever seen.

At exactly the same moment as Hiccup sat down suddenly, gazing at the limpet, there was the faint clear sound of a whistle being blown not far away.

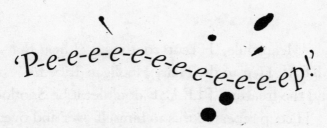

'P-e-e-e-e-e-e-e-e-e-ep!'

'Useless,' said Hiccup, staring at the limpet.
'I really am USELESS. This is the second time the
Gods have sent me a sign. The first time they sent
me a minuscule dragon three times smaller than
anyone else's...'

'Thank you,' said Toothless, staring down into
the hole. 'D-a-a-don't understand it. Really DID
smell m-m-m-metal...'

'... THIS time they send me a gigantic limpet.'

'It's the most enormous limpet I've ever seen,'
said Fishlegs in awe. 'I think you may have discovered
a whole new species.'

'Oh brilliant,' said Hiccup sarcastically,
'*that'll* impress the Tribe. They're all such NATURE
LOVERS.'

He was feeling very black.

'A limpet,' said Hiccup, 'HOWEVER big it is,
is only ever a limpet. It's not TREASURE, is it?
I never heard of a saga where the Hero discovers
a new type of mollusc...'

115

'Meanwhile,' Hiccup continued, 'I hear that the REAL Heir to the Hairy Hooligan Tribe has found the treasure. PLEASE don't let it be Snotlout.'

Hiccup repeated this to himself over and over again as they trudged towards the continuous noise of the whistle.

'Please don't let it be Snotlout, PLEASE don't let it be Snotlout, please, *please*, PLEASE don't let it be Snotlout...'

11. THE TREASURE OF GRIMBEARD THE GHASTLY

Of course it was Snotlout who had found the treasure.

There he stood, chest stuck out, nostrils flaring, a big fat smile on his smug face. Fireworm, his dragon, had blown up to nearly twice her size with pride.

He was surrounded by a crowd of Vikings, who were giving him the Hooligan Hoorah: 'SNOT-LOUT SNOT-LOUT SNOT-LOUT, UGH UGH UGH.'

Snotlout grinned even more widely when he saw Hiccup trudging up, trying to look inconspicuous (difficult when you are attended by a friend carrying a gigantic limpet).

'Look what *I've* found, Hiccup,' drawled Snotlout.

Snotlout had found a large wooden chest, very battered and scuffed and thoroughly gnawed by Skullions. It had the words '**PROPERTY OF GRIMBEARD THE GHASTLY. DO NOT OPEN**' written on it in large golden letters.

Hiccup sighed. No chance of it NOT being the treasure, then.

'Righto then,' said Stoick, rubbing his hands together in a businesslike fashion. 'Let's open it.'

Hiccup forgot about shutting up and keeping a low profile.

'Father,' he whispered urgently, 'we can't open it here. Look, it says "DO NOT OPEN" on the front. Remember what happened last time?'

'NONSENSE,' bellowed Stoick, who had never been more disappointed by his son. Why hadn't HE found the treasure? WHAT was his odd-looking friend doing carrying that ridiculously large shell?

Now Baggybum was going to start suggesting that Snotlout was the rightful Heir to the Tribe, and then Stoick would have to shut him up by fighting him, and it was all Hiccup's fault.

'Of course we open it NOW. What's the point of looking for treasure if you can't open the box when you find it?'

'Please,' pleaded Hiccup, 'you don't think a cunning old pirate like Grimbeard the Ghastly is going to leave a box lying around without there being some sort of trick to it? It'll be BOOBY-TRAPPED. Look what happened when Alvin opened the coffin in the first place – it chopped off his hand – and then when

we opened it later everybody nearly died of fright…'

Stoick finally lost his temper with his son.

'**WHO** is in charge here, anyway?' he roared.
'*I* am the Chief of the Hairy Hooligans, not you,
you small boy.'

Hiccup flinched.

'Those were coincidences, not **BOOBY-TRAPS**.
And I am not going to lug a great heavy box like this

one all the way home only to find it's full of stones.'

Stoick's eyes were already bright with a strange greedy light that Hiccup had never seen before.

'Good point, Chief,' said Gobber the Belch. 'May I?' Gobber swung his axe way over his head and brought it down on the chains wrapped around the box, snapping them in two.

'Snotlout should open it as HE found it,' said Baggybum the Beerbelly.

Stoick sighed. 'OK then,' he said.

Snotlout proudly stepped forward. This was his big moment.

He shot a nasty look at Hiccup.

'Not a good idea, NOT a good idea, NOT A GOOD IDEA,' said Hiccup and Fishlegs to themselves as Snotlout reached out tattooed muscly arms towards the box…

'Not a good idea, N-N-N-NOT a good idea, NOT A G-G-GOOD IDEA,' said Toothless, closing his eyes as Snotlout slowly lifted up the lid…

cr-e-e-e-e-e-e-e-e-e-e-e-a-k…

PROPERTY OF
Grimbeard the Ghastly
DO NOT, I repeat,
DO NOT OPEN THIS BOX
If you do, you will regret it...
BARBARRIANS ROOL OK
THIS WAY UP

12. ESCAPE FROM THE ISLE OF THE SKULLIONS

The chest was not full of stones.

It was full to the brim with a gorgeous treasure. Strings of jewels, golden cups, objects more dazzlingly bright than anything the Hooligans had ever seen before.

'Is it s-s-s-safe to look n-n-n-ow?' asked Toothless, still with his eyes shut.

Hiccup opened his eyes. 'I think so,' he said uncertainly.

He had drawn his sword as Snotlout opened the chest, and now he peered in.

'It seems,' he said suspiciously, 'it seems to be just a box full of treasure.'

'OF COURSE it is,' said Stoick. 'What did I tell you? No BOOBY-TRAPS. You have too much imagination, my boy. Sometimes you have to leave things to the experience of your elders and betters.'

Snotlout had already reached in and drawn out a truly magnificent sword, the scabbard richly decorated with dragons, skulls and the waves of an angry sea.

THAT was a sword fit for a Pirate King. It made the soft hiss of a serpent as Snotlout gently drew it out of the scabbard, and as the sunlight glinted on the still-bright, cruel blade, you could see how bitingly sharp it was, even after all these years underground.

On the handle was a furious portrait of Thor the Thunderer with a tangled seaweedy beard, and across the blade was a zig-zag lightning pattern in a lighter silver.

'The Stormblade...' breathed Baggybum the Beerbelly.

It was, indeed, the Stormblade, Grimbeard the Ghastly's famous sword, with which he had ruled over the entire Inner Isles in such a ruthless fashion.

As Snotlout waved it gently to and fro, it seemed to give off a fierce, hungry light of its own.

Gently, Stoick reached over and took it from his nephew.

'MINE, I think you'll find,' said Stoick calmly. 'The Stormblade belongs to the CHIEF of the Hairy Hooligans, and to him ALONE.'

There was a crafty, greedy look in his eye as he threw aside his own sword and took hold of the Stormblade.

Toothless wrinkled his snout and sniffed.

'What's that s-s-s-s-smell?'

'What smell?' asked Hiccup.

'THAT smell,' replied Newtsbreath, making a face.

Hiccup looked across at Fireworm, the greatest sniffer of them all. The normally flame-red dragon was drooping on Snotlout's shoulder, an extraordinary shade of pale green.

'Suffering scallops!' shouted Hiccup, 'The Skullions!!! SHUT THE BOX!' and he launched himself at the box lid, trying to shut it.

'The boy's gone crazy,' said Baggybum the Beerbelly, easily preventing Hiccup from shutting it by holding it open with one massive forefinger.

'Crazy with jealousy,' sneered Snotlout.

'SHUT THE BOX! SHUT THE BOX! SHUT THE BOX!' yelled Hiccup, struggling in Baggybum's arms.

'Now, now, my boy,' said Stoick, irritated, but trying to soothe his son, 'you can find some treasure NEXT time, I'm sure. We're quite safe, the Skullions can't see us or hear us...'

'But they can SMELL us!' shouted Hiccup. 'GRIMBEARD HAS BOOBY-TRAPPED THE BOX WITH A SMELL THAT WILL WAKE THE SKULLIONS!!!'

'What do you mean, smell us?' asked Stoick.

He gave an experimental sniff. Now the stench was so strong even the humans were noticing it. Fireworm had already thrown up in the heather. All the Hooligans started sniffing, and there it was, an unmistakeable reek of rotting fish and long-dead walrus... with perhaps a hint of month-old crabmeat.

'POOH,' murmured the Hooligans, their attention wandering from the treasure.

'SHUT... THE... BOX!' yelled Hiccup, purple in the face from fury at their stupidity. Light dawned on Stoick the Vast's stupid countenance.

'Ahhhhh... I see what you mean... SHUT THE BOX. Quickly, quickly!' At last he realised the urgency of the situation and shut the box, sitting on it for good measure.

But it made no difference.

The smell was getting stronger by the minute, an unimaginably horrid stench.

If the Skullions caught just one WHIFF of that horrible smell it wouldn't take long for them to wake up and... the thought was too awful to contemplate.

And then Hiccup realised that the awful scritch-scratch of the sleep-sharpening had stopped... and that meant... that meant...

'R-R-R-U-U-U-U-U-U-U-U-U-N!' shouted
Hiccup.

At exactly the same moment Fireworm shrieked,
'D-E-S-E-R-R-R-R-R-R-R-R-T!'

'Let's get out of here,' said Stoick the Vast. He
and Gobber the Belch carried the box together. The
Hooligans didn't need the order. They were already
running as fast as they could towards the beach where
the boats were…

'Leave the box here, Father,' panted Hiccup as he jogged along beside his father. 'They'll go for the box, not us.'

'NO WAY,' said Stoick, his eyes still shining with that glow Hiccup hadn't seen before. 'Think of Alvin's disappointment. Besides, this is my chance for GREATNESS,' he huffed, knocking over a big tower of limpets as he blundered along.

'You are great ALREADY, Father,' urged Hiccup, 'you don't need this treasure...'

But Stoick wouldn't leave it behind.

As they passed the burrows Hiccup could begin to hear horrible snuffling noises coming from inside.

He ran a bit faster.

His heart pounding in terror, he bounded through the heather and crashed through the ferns, at one point falling flat on his face.

The smell was now so strong that it was becoming visible, drifting out of the dents and cracks Gobber had made in the chest in a thick greeny-yellow vapour.

The cliffs of the beach were in sight. They had passed the last mound of Skullions. Maybe they would make it after all.

And then Hiccup heard a noise that made his stomach turn double-somersaults in terror. The noise of animals like big dogs or lions padding behind him, bounding through the heather.

'R-r-r-r-r-r-run!' shrieked Toothless, who was flying three or four feet above Hiccup's head.

Hiccup, Fishlegs, Stoick and Gobber were trailing behind the others, Hiccup and Fishlegs because they were not fast runners, Stoick and Gobber because they were hampered by the box they were carrying.

So they'll get us first, thought Hiccup.

The Skullions were now so close behind them that they could hear the horrible snotty snuffling noises they were making in their noses and the clicking of their teeth.

Hiccup reached the brow of the dunes and launched himself off it in a huge jump on to the sand below. He landed OK, but tripped over his too-large Stretchapoint sword. He rolled over on to his back to look up at the ghastly sight of a gigantic slobbering Skullion, claws outstretched, leaping right on top of him. Its great head was just inches above Hiccup's face.

It was the most dreadful thing Hiccup had ever seen, and it would give him nightmares until he was an old, old, man. It was a face that wasn't a face, no eyes and ears, just that vast nose and slobbering mouth, punctuated by sparkling silver teeth. Black saliva dripped down on to Hiccup's face in a disgusting dribble. The Skullion was holding him down with one clawed paw, while he sniffed down the rest of his body, searching for the tendon in his ankles, the sunlight glinting on that one ludicrously overgrown talon…

Hiccup fumbled for his sword, but the Stretchapoint had fallen out of reach.

Hiccup opened his mouth to shout for help, but no noise came out.

'Help me,' he mouthed soundlessly. 'HELP ME.'

Somebody appeared from nowhere, grabbed the Skullion around the throat, and killed it with one blow from his sword.

It was Stoick the Vast.

The strange grip the treasure had on Stoick loosened as soon as he saw his son's life was in danger.

He left Baggybum the Beerbelly to carry the chest to the ship. He was holding the Stormblade in his right hand and an axe in his left.

'MOVE!!!' yelled Stoick the Vast.

Hiccup moved. He stumbled across the sand.

He could hear more of the creatures bounding after him.

I'm not... going... to... make it... to the boats in time, he thought to himself.

There was a hollow tree trunk sunk into the sand in front of him.

'Climb under the t-t-tree! Climb under the tree!' screeched Toothless.

Hiccup scrambled under it in the nick of time. He could hear a Skullion's jaws clanging together just as he pulled his ankle through the dip in the sand below the tree.

The Skullion was too large to follow him but it pushed its revolting quivering nose through the gap and it started to gnaw at the wood around the hole.

Hiccup grabbed a bone lying on the ground and shoved it as hard as he could up one gigantic nostril.

The Skullion fell back with a howl of anguish.

There was a sickening crash from above as a Skullion landed on top of the tree... and then another... and another... Hiccup could hear horrible scratchings as they worried away with their teeth, trying to break through the wood.

Way above that, Toothless was screaming continuously, 'H-h-help! Help! H-H-H-H-HELP!'

Hiccup swiped at another nose appearing at the hole...

All around him at the edges of the tree trunk he could hear the scrabbling sound of creatures digging through the sand.

It was only a question of time before one of them broke through...

Through a crack at eye level Hiccup could see his father fighting his way towards him up the beach. His dragon hadn't deserted him. Noble Newtsbreath was recklessly tearing into the back of a Skullion three times larger than himself that was about to leap at Stoick.

C-R-U-N-C-C-C-C-C-C-C-C-C H

A Skullion talon pierced the tree trunk, so close to Hiccup that it grazed his chest as it went through.

The head and shoulders of the Skullion appeared in the gaping hole the talon had made. It opened its jaws so wide Hiccup could see right down its black throat.

Hiccup screamed and fell backwards.

Just as the creature lunged forwards to kill him, Hiccup was grabbed around the ankle by one of Stoick's hairy hands, and pulled back through the hole he had climbed in.

Stoick dragged him out, and lifted him up.

'Put your arms up!' bellowed Stoick.

Newtsbreath, hovering overhead, took hold of Hiccup's arms with his talons and carried him up into the air. Toothless grabbed one leg, struggling to help.

Newtsbreath spread out his great wings to their fullest extent.

The Skullions chased after them as they flew, leaping up to bite at Hiccup like dogs after a titbit. Newtsbreath groaned with the strain of trying to get enough height to keep Hiccup out of range of their snapping jaws.

Every now and then, the effort became too much for him, and to Hiccup's terror, he plunged suddenly downwards towards the beach. There was

one very close call when Hiccup
swung his body out of the way just in
time as one of the monsters made a
tremendous leap and nearly took his
legs off at the knee.

By the time they got to the sea,
Newtsbreath's strength had gone,
and Hiccup's ankles were dragging
in the water.

But they were safe.

Skullions cannot swim, and
they loathe the water.

A few more beats of Newtsbreath's
wings, and he dropped Hiccup sprawling
on the deck of the *Lucky Thirteen*. He then
whirled round wearily, and flapped back
to try and help his Master.

Stoick was doing surprisingly well without his help, considering he was fighting a lone battle against increasing numbers of Skullions. Normally, this would have resulted in one dead Chief in about ten seconds flat. You have to remember that Stoick was forty and very, very fat.

But with the Stormblade in his hand, Stoick seemed to have been transformed.

He was awesome.

Yelling the spine-chilling Hooligan Yell, eyes crazy with blood-lust, he performed the 'Fighting Against Superior Numbers Manoeuvre' with spectacular success.

This is a highly complicated Pirate Fighting Skill that only the most co-ordinated and brilliant fighters can carry out.

The pirate takes the Double-Headed Supa-Axe in his left hand and whirls it around his head in a continuous circle that the enemies are unable to penetrate without getting their heads chopped off. At the same time, with the right hand the pirate lunges out of the defensive circle with his sword to attack the enemy.

As you can imagine if you have ever tried to

rub your stomach with one hand while patting your head with the other, this Attacking-while-Defending Skill can only be carried out by the most brilliant and co-ordinated of Vikings.

Skullion after Skullion fell down dead around Stoick as he walked slowly forwards. But a continuous shining wave of the Creatures had poured on to the beach and were cutting off his route to the boats. It seemed impossible that he could make it through the sheer mass of them all, and Newtsbreath, though flying as hard as he could, was still too far away to be any help.

And then, to the complete astonishment of the watching Hooligans, their corpulent, creaky old Leader leapt on to the BACK of the nearest Skullion. The creature madly twisted and bucked, trying to throw him off, but Stoick held on grimly, gripping with his powerful thighs alone, so that he could reach down to right and left, dispatching Skullions with sword and axe.

He cut his way through the mob, riding the maddened beast right into the sea, for all the world as if he were astride an ancient old broken-in Dragon Steed. When the Creature finally bucked him off

137

in the shallows, he turned the fall into a belly-flop forwards, checked for a moment to stow away the sword and the axe, and swam like fury for the boat.

The whole wide bay, and the immediate horizon, was now filled with thousands and thousands of these beasts from hell. It was like a vision out of your worst nightmare.

But the Skullions stopped at the water's edge, and stayed there howling and shrieking furiously. So angry were they that they started turning on the weaker members of their pack, and a few of the creatures were ripped to pieces in front of Hiccup's eyes.

The Hooligans cheered and cheered and cheered.

Stoick was very pleased with himself.

He acknowledged the frantic applause, wiped the blood off the Stormblade on to his shirt, and kissed the clean blade.

And then he threw back his hairy head and ROARED like an animal, and so wild did he look with the sword in his hand and the blood on his shirt, that Hiccup barely recognised his own father.

13. THE ARGUMENT

The graze on Hiccup's chest was actually deeper than he had realised in the terror of the moment. It would leave a scar that would stay with him for the rest of his life as a reminder of a morning spent on the Isle of the Skullions.

And his right arm was dislocated from the strain of hanging from the talons of Newtsbreath. Gobber put it back in its socket (a very painful process, as Gobber was not the most tender of nurses) and tore a strip off his shirt to make Hiccup a sling for it.

The Hooligans gave themselves a couple of minutes to pat each other on the back and celebrate, before grabbing the oars again. They were eager to leave the spooky Isle of the Skullions far, far behind them. It wasn't until they were within sight of the friendly cliffs of Berk that they felt safe enough to ship their oars, and let the *Lucky Thirteen* drift for a while in calm but misty seas while they investigated their prize.

When Stoick lifted the lid of the box again, the smell had nearly gone. But underneath the treasure there was a scattering of greenish-yellow crystals which appeared to be smoking slightly, and they still gave off that rotten-egg stench. These were what Grimbeard had used to booby-trap the box – as soon as they came into contact with the air they let off their smell, which then alerted the Skullions.

A very effective and deadly defence of his treasure.

And **WHAT** a treasure it was... Alvin could not speak for at least three minutes. He just stood there, eyes popping, picking up object after object and stroking it, letting his hands run lovingly through the coins.

'Of course, ten per cent of this treasure shall be yours, Alvin,' boomed Stoick the Vast, sticking his belly out in pride at his own generosity.

'You are *tooooo* kind, dearest Stoick,' murmured Alvin, when he could say anything at all.

'Hang on an oyster-catching minute,' interrupted Baggybum the Beerbelly. 'Firstly, I want it acknowledged that SNOTLOUT found this treasure.'

'Acknowledged,' said Stoick the Vast reluctantly.

Hiccup knew he should be thankful to be alive, but he was unspeakably miserable. He knew what all this was going to mean. Hiccup, although the

son of the Chief, was not the True Heir to the
Hairy Hooligans. The True Heir was Snotlout,
who had always been bigger, faster and more brilliant
at everything than Hiccup.

'Secondly,' continued Baggybum, 'as the
FINDER OF THE TREASURE, technically it
belongs to MY SON Snotlout, and I don't know
whether Snotlout feels like giving away any of
it to some stranger...'

'He definitely doesn't,' grinned Snotlout.

Stoick the Vast banged shut the treasure chest.
He lifted Baggybum the Beerbelly clear off the
ground by the front of his shirt, which was quite some
feat considering Baggybum the Beerbelly was about
the size of a killer whale who hadn't taken much
exercise recently.

'I AM THE CHIEF OF THIS TRIBE!'
roared Stoick the Vast. 'I LAUNCHED THIS
EXPEDITION TO FIND THE TREASURE
OF GRIMBEARD THE GHASTLY AND
THIS TREASURE BELONGS TO ME AND
ME ALONE!'

Baggybum the Beerbelly gave Stoick a quick jab
in the kidney, which made Stoick drop him, sharpish.

He yelled right back in Stoick's face:

'WELL MAYBE YOU'VE BEEN CHIEF
OF THIS TRIBE A LITTLE TOO LONG, BIG
BROTHER! MAYBE THIS IS A SIGN FROM
THE GODS THAT IT'S TIME YOU RETIRED.
WHAT DID THAT PROPHECY SAY ABOUT
THE HEIR FINDING THE TREASURE? IF
MY SON IS THE HEIR, MAYBE THAT JUST
MAKES ME THE CHIEF OF THE TRIBE
INSTEAD OF YOU!!!'

'NO!' yelled Stoick, stamping his foot, 'I'M THE CHIEF!'

'ARE NOT!'

'AM TOO!'

They had grabbed each other by the shoulders and were carrying out a Staring Contest, the horns on their helmets locked together like a couple of rutting stags.

'Neff off,' said Stoick, with quiet and sinister emphasis.

'No, YOU neff off,' replied Baggybum.

'No, YOU neff off.'

'YOU!'

'YOU!' etc. etc. etc.

While all this was going on, nobody noticed Alvin doing something rather strange.

When the *Lucky Thirteen* sailed into easy flying distance of the cliffs of Berk, most of the dragons had flown off back to the Hooligan Village, for food and rest. The only one who had remained on the *Lucky Thirteen* was Toothless. Toothless, who was a lazy little creature, considered this was too far to fly. And he had caught himself a couple of nice plump mackerel on the way. So, there he still was, on the deck, watching the fight with interest.

For some strange reason of his own, Alvin picked up a heavy empty barrel. He placed it over the excited little dragon, trapping him underneath.

He then interrupted the fight between Stoick and Baggybum.

'Now, now,' said Alvin soothingly, 'little clams in their shells agree. This should be a JOYFUL moment, the beginning of a glorious new era for the Hooligan Tribe. There is plenty of treasure for all of you. I propose a toast to celebrate the finding of the treasure.'

The Hooligans cheered, hoping to get over a difficult moment. Gobber and Hugefarts pulled Stoick and Baggybum apart, because otherwise they were clearly prepared to stand there all day. Some of the other Hooligan Warriors handed out blackcurrant wine for the toast.

Stoick the Vast drew the Stormblade. He had already decked himself out in some fancy earrings from the treasure chest.

'Half-wits and HEROES,' he shouted. 'We, a small band of unbeatable barbarians, are about to become the centre of a New Empire, an Empire

to rival Rome in her glory days! With this treasure,'
Stoick lifted his cup of blackcurrant wine, his eyes
glittering, 'the Hairy Hooligans shall become
INVINCI—'

14. THE DAY TAKES A TURN FOR THE WORSE

Stoick never finished the word 'invincible' because halfway through he was grabbed around the neck by an enormous wild-eyed individual and a not very clean knife was held to his neck. So the word ended up more like 'INVINCI-*ugh-ugh-ugh*', as Stoick choked and his eyes popped.

All around the rowing benches every Hooligan aboard had been grabbed from behind and knives were held at every throat.

The Hooligans' nerves were still jangling from the flight from the Skullions. And they had been so busy arguing that they hadn't spotted a small sleek boat sneaking up through the mist and drawing alongside the *Lucky Thirteen*. A boat named the *Hammerhead* with a sail curved like a shark's fin and a red skull and crossbones painted on the side. A boat packed to the brim with OUTCASTS.

They were not a pretty crew, despite their height, and their handsome red hair, and their gorgeous clothes, and every kind of golden ornament. Many had

scars carved into their faces. One or two were
without a nose or an ear. Most had filed their teeth
into sharp little points, like the teeth of a shark.
Even the good-looking ones were disfigured by
dark red tattoos, said to be made out of the blood

of their enemies. They talked to each other in the most difficult of Viking languages, Outcastese, which sounds very much like the barking of a dog.

The Outcasts had swarmed over the side and crept up behind the Hooligans as they were admiring the Treasure and themselves. Toothless had smelt them, of course. He knew they were coming and he had been going crazy inside the big heavy barrel, shrieking at the top of his voice, 'OUTCASTS! R-R-RUN FOR YOUR LIVES, YOU S-S-S-STUPID H-H-HUMANS!!!'

But nobody had heard him.

All in all, this was turning into a very bad day for the Hooligans. Outcasts, like Skullions, are the kind of creature one really hopes one can live a lifetime without bumping into, let alone seeing BOTH of them at close quarters in the space of one morning.

Hiccup did not realise they were Outcasts. But he knew they were Bad Trouble.

His heart started jumping in his chest like a mudskipper as he looked into the terrible face of the man who had Stoick the Vast by the throat. His curly horns were quite three feet high. When he opened his mouth he growled like a dog.

This is Outcastese, and it translates roughly as 'Got him! What do we do now, Chief ??'

For a whole minute, nobody said a word. Nobody dared move a muscle. There was no noise at all except for that terrible dog-like growling from the Outcast who was holding Stoick… and the sound of Alvin drinking.

There was no knife at Alvin's throat.

Calmly, he finished off the last delicious drops of blackcurrant wine. Smoothly, he put the cup down.

'I thought that I would provide a – ah – surprise ending to our little journey,' said Alvin, with his charming smile. 'I DO like surprises, don't you, my dear Stoick?'

Stoick gargled inarticulately.

'Such fun, aren't they?' continued Alvin. 'I am so sorry to say, however, that the day of glory for the Hooligan Tribe may be – ah – put off for a while. You see, I feel that I ought to have rather more than a mere ten per cent. And in case you didn't agree I thought I would bring along some of my relatives to – ah – persuade you to give it up.'

Stoick gargled again.

Alvin barked out a few words in Outcastese to Curly Horns, who barked back at him again.

'I have to admit at this point that I have been guilty of a little innocent deception,' said Alvin. 'My name is not Alvin the Poor-But-Honest-Farmer. I am, in fact, His Most Mighty Murderousness Alvin the Treacherous, Great High Chieftain of the Outcast Tribe. I don't know why, but I felt that if I had told you this from the beginning you might not have given me a very warm welcome.'

'An OUTCAST?' gasped the Hooligans.

Alvin laughed. 'That's right,' he said, 'an Outcast. Us Outcasts don't always go around on all fours dressed in animal skins, you know. Even *we* are moving with the times.' He went over to Stoick and gently removed the Stormblade from Stoick's hand.

'MINE, I think,' said Alvin.

Alvin unscrewed the claw from his right hand, as Hiccup had seen him do once before. He attached his 'sword-holder' contraption in its place, into which he carefully twisted the Stormblade. He screwed it very tightly, so that it was completely steady. And while he did all this, he talked.

'You see, Stoick,' said Alvin, 'we Barbarian Chieftains are facing a new challenge. We have to fight the creeping forces of Civilisation by becoming FIERCER and CRUELLER than ever. YOU, Stoick, have GONE SOFT.'

'I have NOT!' protested Stoick indignantly.

'Grimbeard the Ghastly would be turning in his grave if he could see you now,' tut-tutted Alvin. 'You Hooligans have become bungling AMATEURS, all noise and show with no real wickedness to you at all. Now, *I* have worked hard to bring us Outcasts up to date. Outwardly, we now have some of the clothes and the manners of Civilisation… but inwardly we are tougher and more truly Outcast than we have ever been. We are your REAL PROFESSIONAL PIRATES, heartless, murdering, bloodsucking, slave-traders…' Alvin paused for breath.

The Most High and Murderous Alvin the Treacherous

'Talking of which,' he then continued,
'take your last look at your rather plain little island…'
He gestured at the friendly cliffs of Berk. 'All of
you Hooligans are about to enter the slave trade
yourselves, in the very important role of SLAVES.'

The Hooligans groaned. There was no worse
fate for a proud and independent Viking than to be
sold into bondage.

'I am sure you will all make excellent slaves,'
said Alvin kindly, 'because you are all very strong, and,
frankly, none too bright. And I do hate to threaten, but
anybody who objects will thoroughly regret it.'

An Outcast with no nose stepped forward and
uncurled an ugly black whip from around his waist,
with a handle shaped like a serpent.

Alvin clapped his hands and the Outcasts
began loading the Hooligans on to the deck of
the *Hammerhead*.

'Yup, you shall all be slaves. All that is…'
smiled Alvin, '… except for you, Stoick.'

Curly Horns let Stoick go, and proudly, he
stepped forward.

'To Chieftains and their descendants we pay
the ultimate sign of respect,' said Alvin with just
a tiny hint of menace in his voice, 'by EATING them.'

'But that's CANNIBALISM,' said Stoick,
shocked.

'I know, I know,' sighed Alvin. 'It's very old-
fashioned of me, but I would lose respect in front
of the rest of my Tribe if I dropped ALL the old
traditions…'

'But… but… but… but…' blustered Stoick.

'I shall not change my mind, whatever you say,'
said Alvin gently. 'The thing about dinner is, it never
wants to be eaten. I mean, you eat PORK, don't you,
Stoick?'

'Well, yeees,' admitted Stoick.

'There you are then!' said Alvin. 'No pig is ever
going to VOLUNTEER to be supper, and, thinking of
volunteers…' Something seemed to be amusing Alvin.
He giggled delightedly. 'I mentioned that it would not
only be Stoick who would receive this, ah… honour,'

said Alvin, 'but also his descendants. I know there has been some sort of argument about this recently. The question is,' continued Alvin, struggling to keep a straight face, 'WHO is the Heir to Stoick the Vast? Could they put up their hand please?'

Strangely enough, Snotlout did not put up his hand at this point.

Instead, he tried to hide behind Dogsbreath the Duhbrain, staring very hard at his bronze-tipped sandals, as if he hadn't quite heard the question.

Hiccup sighed.

He stood right up on the bench so that everyone could see him.

'I,' said Hiccup, 'I am the Heir to Stoick the Vast.'

Stoick smiled a big, proud smile.

For all their manners, the Outcasts whispered a great deal at that. Hiccup didn't have to speak Outcastese to know that they were saying things like: '*That* skinny prawn is the Heir to the Hairy Hooligans???'

Two gigantic Outcasts lifted Hiccup from the bench and set him down next to Stoick the Vast.

Alvin held up the Stormblade. The sword was

Outcastese for
'That skinny prawn
is the Heir to the
Hairy Hooligans??'

now just an extension of his arm, like the horn of
a narwhal is an extension of its nose.

'It looks as if it has always been there, doesn't it?'
said Alvin.

The daylight played across the bolt of lightning
motif. Alvin drew a finger across the blade ever so
lightly, and blood instantly dropped on to the deck.

'Nice and sharp. This won't take a second,'
promised Alvin, stepping towards Hiccup.

15. THE BATTLE ON BOARD THE LUCKY THIRTEEN

Alvin advanced towards Hiccup, with the Stormblade raised above his head.

Hiccup closed his eyes, waiting for the blow.

But at that moment Toothless finally managed to overturn the barrel he was trapped underneath.

He had been throwing his entire body weight at one side for the past five minutes. At last he made an extra-strong he-*e-e-eave*, the barrel tipped over, and rolled at great speed across the deck with Toothless rumbling round and round inside it... and bowled straight into the legs of Alvin the Treacherous... who lost his footing and fell over...

Alvin gave an *ooohh* of surprise, the Outcasts were distracted for one vital second, and Stoick turned round and felled Curly Horns with a good old-fashioned upper cut right under the chin.

From that moment on, there was chaos aboard the *Lucky Thirteen*.

The Hooligans took advantage of their captors' surprise as the swords against their throats were lowered for a moment.

'THIS IS MORE LIKE IT! I'LL TEACH YOU TO SAY THE HOOLIGANS HAVE GONE SOFT!!!!' Stoick let out the Viking War Cry and launched himself on the enemy completely bare-handed. He crashed two Outcasts' heads together, jabbed another in the kidney with his foot, and when that one doubled over in pain, leapfrogged over his back to face another couple of the opposition.

All might not have gone well for him, however, unarmed as he was, if Baggybum the Beerbelly had not come to his aid. The two brothers, who had been fighting each other five minutes earlier, now fought the enemy back-to-back for the rest of the battle.

The 'Battle on Board the *Lucky Thirteen*' would be a Saga that the Hooligans would tell their

children and grandchildren for many, many years
to come. The military prowess of the Outcast Tribe
was legendary throughout the Viking World. But
the Hooligans were desperate and angry. They were
battling for their FREEDOM itself, and so fought more
wildly, more fiercely, than perhaps they had
ever done before or since.

No fewer than twenty Black Stars* were
awarded to Warriors after the battle was over.
No wonder, for the Pirate Fighting Skills on display
on that occasion were a joy to watch. They were also
a tribute to the old soldier, Gobber, who had taught
most of the Warriors all that they knew. There, on one
corner of the deck, was Nobber Nobrains, performing
the highly skilled manoeuvre known as the 'Dance
of the Axes', in which the pirate rapidly juggles two
twirling axes from one hand to the other, hypnotising
and confusing the enemy, before the pirate lunges
forward for the fatal blow.

Up around the mast were the boys from the
Pirate Training Programme, valiantly tackling Outcasts
nearly twice their size, putting into practice all that

---

* The 'Black Star' was a medal given to Hooligan Warriors for Outstanding
Bravery in the Field of Combat.

Fishlegs goes
BESERK

162

they had learnt during those Swordfighting at Sea
lessons.

The behaviour of Fishlegs was particularly
surprising. As soon as the battle began, he completely
lost control, throwing himself at the enemy, shrieking
furiously and whirling his sword around his head
like a madman.

Vikings call this 'going Beserk' and Warriors who
do this are revered in Viking society.

You could not imagine a more unlikely candidate
for being a Beserk than Fishlegs, but there we are,
these things are never predictable.

The Outcasts stayed out of his way, for a Beserk
is always respected, even if he is only four foot ten
with a squint and a limp and no swordfighting skills
whatsoever.

It has to be admitted (reluctantly), that Snotlout
fought with spectacular brilliance and bravery. His
quick wrist made the Flashcut slip neatly in and
out, hither and thither, beautifully performing the
Destroyer's Defence, the Grimbeard's Grapple,
the Final Cut, and many, many more of the subtlest
swordfighting skills. In the space of five minutes
no fewer than three Outcasts lay dead around him,

all much larger and heavier than himself. This is a schoolboy record that stands to this day.

I would love to say that Hiccup fought similarly splendidly. But I can't, because it wouldn't be true. Hiccup had dislocated his arm, remember, and his sword, the Stretchapoint, lay somewhere on the beach at the Isle of the Skullions. But Hiccup did what he could. With his quick left hand he picked a key out of Curly Horns' pocket while he fought Gobber the Belch. He used the key to unlock the chains of four or five Hooligans who had already been bound, ready for slavery, who then joined in the fight with the others.

Toothless created an extra diversion when he spilled out of the barrel, dizzy and confused, and bit the first hairy leg that he saw. Which happened to belong to a grossly fat Outcast, who promptly dropped the flare he had been carrying right in the open barrel of blackcurrant wine.

And Thor only knows what was IN that blackcurrant wine, but the entire barrel burst into flames.

The fire raged out of control.

The sail burned furiously, and thick black smoke poured over the deck.

Everybody started jumping off the *Lucky Thirteen* in order to escape the flames.

Stoick belly-flopped into the sea, and splashed over to the Outcast boat, the *Hammerhead*, where the pitched battle was continuing. As he climbed over the side of the *Hammerhead*, he turned back to his son and shouted, 'Come ON, Hiccup!'

'Your f-f-f-father's right,' panted Toothless, 'w-w-we should go.'

Hiccup hesitated.

Fishlegs was still aboard the *Lucky Thirteen*.

He was in the grip of the Beserk trance, and was following Alvin, sword in hand, hoping to kill him.

The Hammerhead

Alvin had turned back to fetch the treasure.

'FISHLEGS!' yelled Hiccup desperately. 'WE'VE GOT TO GET OFF THE BOAT!'

But Fishlegs couldn't hear him.

'FISHLEGS!' shouted Hiccup, hesitating some more, 'IF WE DON'T GET OFF NOW WE MAY BE TOO LATE!'

It was already too late.

There was a mighty C-R-E-E-E-E-E-E-E-E-E-E-A-A-A-K!!!!!! from above and the burning mast crashed into the sea.

Stoick watched in horror from the deck of the *Hammerhead* as the *Lucky Thirteen* flipped over on to its back, trapping Hiccup, Fishlegs, Alvin and Toothless underneath it as it did so.

It then sank before his eyes.

And Stoick knew that this particular part of the ocean, despite being so close to the cliffs, was very, very deep, too deep even for lobster pots.

'HIC-CUP!' yelled Stoick in despair.

He knew that he would never see his son again.

For who could get out of *that* situation alive?

16. AT THE BOTTOM OF THE OCEAN

Hiccup's first thought was that he was going to drown. He was turned over and over in somersault after somersault, down, down, down in such a rush that he felt like his head was bursting. A strange, calm sensation of no longer really caring came over him, and then he was roughly grabbed by the shoulders and dragged coughing and spluttering to the surface of the water and into an air-pocket trapped beneath the sinking ship.

The boat was still travelling downwards with such rapidity that Hiccup's ears popped again and again, but at least he could breathe.

'My turn to save YOUR life,' gasped Fishlegs.

'Oh, yes,' said Hiccup sarcastically, once he'd got his breath back, 'and I suppose the reason I'm here in the first place is nothing to do with you? If you hadn't gone rushing after Alvin we would be on board the other boat by now... Didn't you hear me shouting at you?'

Fishlegs blushed. 'Couldn't hear anything,

actually,' he mumbled.

'A fine time for us to
discover you're a Beserk,'
grumbled Hiccup.

Fishlegs blushed even deeper.
'Do you think that's what it was?' he asked shyly.
He was secretly extremely proud that he had these
violent hidden depths.

'Yes, I do,' said Hiccup. 'Anyway, my life isn't
exactly SAVED yet, is it? It's not like we're tucked
up safely in bed in the Hooligan Village. I mean, where
ARE we?'

The boat finally stopped its descent and settled
gently on the sea-bed.

'At the b-b-b-bottom of the ocean,'
said Toothless, as he floated by, crouched in
an upturned Outcast helmet like a malevolent
eagle sitting on a nest, his eyes glowing like
candles. (One of the only interesting features of
the Common or Garden dragon is that its eyes light
up in the dark.)

'The boat turned over and we seem

to be trapped underneath in some sort of air-pocket,'
explained Fishlegs.

Hiccup peered up the length of the upturned
Lucky Thirteen. Sure enough, all the benches were
now the ceiling of what looked like a long, low, barrel
vaulted hall, with water for a floor. Chairs, oars,
cushions floated by, but as far as he could see or hear,
there was no one else trapped with them, no furious
Outcasts or helpful Hooligans.

'Everyone else must have jumped
off in time,' said Fishlegs.

'Hang on a sec,' said Hiccup, 'somebody
seems to be stuck under a bench down there...'
He dived below the surface, his kicking legs swamping
Fishlegs and Toothless in a small tidal wave.

He was gone for nearly a minute and a half.
When he finally resurfaced, he was holding a very limp
and green Alvin the Treacherous.

'What you saving HIM for?' complained
Toothless. 'He a r-r-rat. Toothless kill him,
if you like,' he said, cheering up no end,

his claws extending towards the sleeping Alvin.

As if he heard these words, Alvin opened his eyes. His face crumpled up and he cried like a baby.

'My treasure,' he cried, 'my treasure. Gone, gone, gone...'

'We are not interested in your treasure,' said Fishlegs coldly. 'What about the fact that not half an hour ago you were about to put the entire Hooligan Tribe into slavery? Not to mention serving up poor old Hiccup here as a starter. If it wasn't for YOUR stupid treasure we could all be sitting in one of Gobber the Belch's classes staring vacantly out of the window while he bangs on about Frightening Foreigners.'

'We can still find it,' said Alvin urgently, trying to peer into the water below him. 'It's down there somewhere, the ground isn't far beneath me. HELP ME everybody, and we shall live like kings...'

'Oh belt up, you madman,' snapped Fishlegs.

'We haven't time,' interrupted Hiccup. 'This really is our lucky day. Correct me if I'm wrong, but I think this air-pocket is getting smaller.'

Hiccup was right.

The air-pocket was getting smaller.

17. HOW BAD COULD THIS DAY GET?

The 'ceiling' was definitely nearer to their heads than it had been a few minutes before. It was now just a few inches above the horns on Hiccup's helmet.

There was silence for a second. Alvin's mad eyes swam back into focus again. The only thing that mattered more to him than the treasure was the preservation of his own life.

Hiccup found everyday life rather a trial but was always good in a crisis. 'RIGHT,' he said, 'Toothless, I want you to swim out from under this boat and see whether you think we're too far to swim to the surface. NOW,' he added, as Toothless seemed to be taking his time about it.

'OK, OK,' grumbled Toothless, 'k-k-k-keep your horns on...'

The little dragon dived underneath the water and disappeared. He left the Vikings in nearly total darkness, for without the friendly light of his glowing eyes it was almost impossible to see. There was an eerie silence, apart from the lapping of the water against the sides of the boat, and a faint rushing noise, which Hiccup was sure was the sound of the air leaving the air-pocket like a leaking balloon.

And indeed, after five minutes the air-pocket had reduced so much that Hiccup's head was squashed against the wooden 'ceiling' of *The Lucky Thirteen*, and he had to remove his helmet.

Alvin was panicking. 'Where is the wretched reptile?' he hissed, and then choked as water sloshed into his mouth.

'That wretched reptile,' scolded Fishlegs, as terrified as Alvin but bravely trying not to show it, 'is trying to save *your* wretched life...'

Five minutes more and they had to turn their heads in order to keep their nostrils clear of the water. *If Toothless takes any longer,'* thought Hiccup, *'we're going to drown here in this blackness...*

Two lights flickered in the dark below him. It was Toothless, swimming up towards them in the nick of time.

'OK,' said Toothless. 'Surface t-t-too far away for h-h-h-h-humans... but there's a c-c-c-c-cave thingy... F-f-follow Toothless...'

'Just hang on to me, Fishlegs, and kick like crazy,' ordered Hiccup, because, of course, Fishlegs could not swim.

Hiccup took a huge breath, *just* before the sea swallowed up the last remains of that air-pocket, and dived after Toothless.

He had to swim underneath the rim of the boat, which was resting on some large rocks on the bottom.

He swam out into total darkness, which was very confusing. A little way above him, he could see that Toothless was swimming towards a small hole in

the cliff, with light shining out of it. Trying to ignore
the panicky feeing of his breath running out, and
hampered by Fishlegs gripping on to one leg, he swam
as fast as he could towards the hole. Once he had
swum into it, he shot upwards through a short tunnel
and surfaced in a huge pool of water at the bottom
of a gigantic underground cavern, gasping for air.

A second or so later, Alvin emerged to lie in
the water beside Hiccup and Fishlegs.

The cavern was huge, and surprisingly light,
considering it was so far underground. The eerie green
light seemed to be given off by Electricsquirms, a tiny
dragon-like creature that glows with phosphorescence.
Water rushed down the walls and dripped from
the ceiling.

Hiccup was so relieved to be still alive and in the
air again that this tomb of a cavern initially seemed
like home. It was a while before his scared brain could
focus on the fact that they weren't safe yet.

'Right,' said Fishlegs, trying not to panic and
wringing out his breeches and flapping his arms to
get dry. 'How are we going to get out of HERE?'

The cavern had some interesting rock
formations, if Hiccup had been in the mood for

admiring them. The weird shapes of fossilised dragons were caught in the stone. Some of them were very unusual, extinct species. However, even the discovery of an entire skeleton of the Burrowing Slitherfang, so rare that it was often thought never to have existed, failed to excite Hiccup as it might have done in other circumstances.

They walked round and round in circles for about an hour and a half, looking for a way out, before realising that there wasn't one. They sat down.

Without his Tribe around him, and facing Death, Alvin seemed to have returned to his old, pleasant self again. He even apologised for getting them into this mess.

'I just cannot believe this,' moaned Fishlegs, shivering violently. 'It's like some sort of NIGHTMARE. I keep thinking we're safe, and then it seems that, NO, we're in some OTHER life-threatening situation even worse than the one we've just got away from.'

'OK,' admitted Hiccup, trying to keep them from despairing, 'it doesn't look good, but I'm sure I can think of a way out of here...'

Toothless was sniffing away at the back of

175

the cavern, and he interrupted, calling out, 'Toothless can smell something m-metal over h-h-here!'

'Very clever, Toothless,' said Hiccup, 'but the Treasure Hunt is over now.'

'I mean,' continued Fishlegs, 'so far today we have narrowly escaped being **1.** Torn to pieces by Skullions. **2.** Eaten by Cannibal Outcasts. **3.** Burned to death on board ship. **4.** Drowned at the bottom of the ocean... And now here we are, trapped in an inaccessible underground cavern facing DEATH BY SLOW STARVATION... It's just been a REALLY BAD day.'

'N-n-not metal after all,' Toothless called back in disappointment. 'It's just a d-d-door...'

'A DOOR??' Alvin, Hiccup and Fishlegs scrambled up and over towards Toothless, with a sudden surge of hope.

Once they had scrabbled away at all the dust and earth covering it, they found it *was* a door. It was surprising they hadn't noticed it before.

'Is it a way out?' gasped Fishlegs.

'Not necessarily,' Hiccup replied slowly.

A door with a DEATH'S HEAD painted on it. A door with lettering on it that was horribly

familiar to Hiccup.

Large, scrawling letters gouged out of the surface of the wood, probably with a sword.

'DO NOT OPEN THIS DOOR,' it said, 'UNLESS YOU ARE THE TRUE HEIR TO GRIMBEARD THE GHASTLY.

'I REALLY MEAN IT THIS TIME,' it said, 'DEATH AND DESTRUCTION AND OTHER TRULY AWFUL THINGS WILL FOLLOW IF YOU OPEN THIS DOOR. THIS IS A PIRATE'S PRIVATE PERSONAL PROPERTY.'

Hiccup looked straight into the suddenly glittering eyes of Alvin the Treacherous. All the pleasantness had fallen away from him again. He raised his arm with the Stormblade fixed into it.

Alvin didn't need to say anything.

Hiccup knew what he wanted.

'Ohhhhh no,' said Hiccup, backing slowly away, 'I'm not going to open this door.'

'Oh, but you *are*,' smiled Alvin the Treacherous, resting the point of the Stormblade right in the centre of Hiccup's chest.

'But I'm not the Heir to Grimbeard the Ghastly,' Hiccup protested. 'Snotlout is the Heir. He's the one who found the treasure, remember the riddle?'

'Ah, but was that the *real* treasure that Snotlout found?' asked Alvin. 'Perhaps Grimbeard put it there as a decoy, to make people think they'd found the real treasure, when all along it was lying here. What better hiding place than a cavern accessible only by water? And if that wasn't the real treasure, that means Snotlout isn't necessarily the True Heir to the Hairy Hooligans.'

you are the Heir to Grimbeard the Ghastly

'Well, that's a relief, in any case,' said Fishlegs, trying to lighten the tension.

'YOU are the True Heir,' said Alvin quietly. 'When I asked on the *Lucky Thirteen* who was the Heir to the Hairy Hooligans, who stood up? YOU did. Not Snotlout. This has all been a Test, set by Grimbeard the Ghastly and Fate herself. Only now does the riddle make sense. For what have we just escaped from, but a watery grave?

'And WHOSE Beast has just sniffed out this door? YOUR Beast.'

'S-s-see?' said Toothless. 'Toothless is better s-s-sniffer than Fireworm.'

'YOU are the True Heir to the Hairy Hooligans, Hiccup,' said Alvin. 'And so only YOU can open this door and live.'

'But I don't want to open this door,' said Hiccup. 'If you give me enough time I'm sure I can get us out of here without opening it. What about the booby traps? *You* open Grimbeard's coffin and you lose your right hand... *We* open Grimbeard's treasure chest and it triggers a smell that wakes up the Skullions... I KNOW that if we open this door something REALLY UNPLEASANT is going to happen, sure as fish-eggs are fish-eggs. And the surprises are getting WORSE, if anything.'

'I forgot to mention,' said Alvin silkily, 'if you don't open the door, you DIE.'

He pressed the Stormblade forward a bit so that it pierced the skin just above Hiccup's heart.

'Let me get this straight,' said Hiccup, 'if I do open this door, you WON'T kill me or my friends?'

'I promise,' said Alvin, 'word of a Treacherous.'

'Word of a Treacherous...' groaned Fishlegs. 'It says it all really... He'll kill us as soon as he has the treasure... if there is any treasure behind that door...'

'But otherwise he's going to kill us now,' Hiccup pointed out. 'I haven't got a lot of choice.'

Hiccup leaned forward, biting his lip, and slid the heavy iron bolt to the left.

'NOT a good idea, NOT a good idea, NOT A GOOD IDEA,' repeated Fishlegs and Toothless to themselves, closing their eyes.

Hiccup slow-ly opened the door...

cr-e-e-e-e-e-e-e-e-e-e-e-e-a-k...

Alvin, Fishlegs, Hiccup and Toothless stood there, their mouths flopping open and shut like fish in their astonishment.

The door had opened on to another GIGANTIC cavern. This was filled to the brim with more treasure than you could possibly imagine in your wildest dreams, even were you as greedy as Alvin himself.

So indescribably beautiful was this treasure that it drew them into the room like a magnet.

It was all piled up on top of itself in crazy giant mountains. Mound after mound of golden coins with Caesar stamped on one side, and Neptune on the other. Heap after heap of rubies fat and ripe as scallops and emeralds green as a mermaid's eye. Gorgeous silver cups with seahorses galloping delicately around them and golden necklaces as plump as oysters and swords as sharp as a conger's tooth with octopus tentacles winding themselves around the hilt.

It was the sort of treasure you could get lost in, and forget yourself and your mind and this world at all.

'Oh my,' breathed Alvin the Treacherous, stepping forward. 'Oh my, my, my...' And he reached out to grasp a cup, a glorious golden goblet, perfectly round in shape, with dolphins playing around the rim, so beautifully carved that it looked as if they were alive and leaping in a miniature golden sea.

Toothless, Hiccup and Fishlegs recollected where they were, and slowly backed towards the open door while Alvin was so preoccupied.

But Alvin caught a glimpse of them out of the corner of his eye, and he stretched out and shut the door with the point of the Stormblade.

'Nobody leaves the cavern without asking Alvin,' he said.

'Now, Alvin,' said Hiccup nervously. 'Remember your promise. If I opened the door, you said you'd let us all live.'

'Ye-e-e-e-s-s-s,' said Alvin, considering the cup again, and then dropping it softly back on the pile. 'The thing is, Outcasts don't always keep promises to other people. I blame our upbringing. My mother never really loved me, you know. But I always keep promises I make to MYSELF. And long ago, when that coffin lid snapped down and chopped off my hand, I made myself a very solemn promise indeed.'

Alvin's pleasant eyes narrowed, and he sidled towards Hiccup like a predatory crab. 'It's not that

I dislike you personally, Hiccup, but I swore to myself,' said Alvin, still smiling, 'that I would FIND Grimbeard's precious Treasure, and I would KILL his precious Heir. That's fair, isn't it, an Heir in exchange for a hand?'

And he made a vicious swipe at Hiccup with the Stormblade.

Hiccup dodged out of the way in the nick of time. He leapt nimbly on to the nearest mound of treasure and started scrambling up it.

'And with Grimbeard's own precious sword, too,' chuckled Alvin. 'Isn't fate ARTISTIC?'

'TOOTHLESS!' yelled Hiccup. 'Get me a SWORD!'

Alvin climbed after him and made another wild lunge at his head.

Hiccup ducked behind a large golden chariot wheel.

'TOOTH-LESS!' cried Hiccup, 'HURRY UP!'

184

'OK, OK,' muttered Toothless, who had flown to a pile of weaponry not far away. 'K-k-keep your helmet on. T-t-toothless doing his BEST.'

Toothless tried to pick up three of the swords, all of them as big and beautiful and flashy as the Stormblade itself. But they were all too heavy.

So he turned to something smaller, an undistinguished but serviceable object, a bit rusty at the edges perhaps. He could lift it easily with both talons, and flew with it to where Hiccup was climbing. He was a quarter of the way up a hill of treasure, hotly pursued by Alvin, who had little red lights dancing in his narrowed eyes and was swishing that Stormblade like he was a human flail.

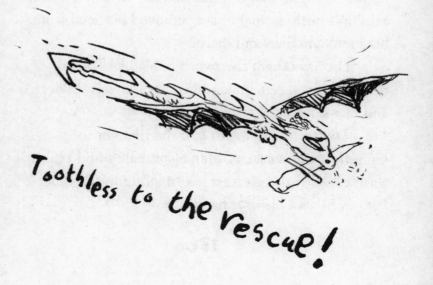

Toothless to the rescue!

Toothless dropped the rusty sword into Hiccup's hand, and he caught it just in time to parry a blow by Alvin so terrible that if it had actually connected with Hiccup's neck, it might have removed his head from his shoulders then and there.

Hiccup caught the sword in his LEFT hand, because, if you remember, his right arm was dislocated and in a sling.

This isn't going to last long, he thought to himself. It was a case of Man against Boy, and Hiccup wasn't exactly the greatest swordfighter in the Inner Isles even with his *right* hand.

'Keep your point UP, Hiccup,' shouted Fishlegs, desperately trying to clamber up after them so he could help. 'Eye on the swords at all times, a strong wrist, remember your footwork...'

Alvin the Treacherous gave a great swipe at Hiccup's belly, and Hiccup was surprised to find his left arm jerk up and his own sword block Alvin's in the nick of time.

Alvin was equally surprised, and he hauled his great sword over his wicked head and he brought it down towards Hiccup's neck, and Hiccup's arm flashed up and parried the blow just before it bit.

Astonished, Alvin began raining blows thick and fast, swiping and slashing and lunging and Hiccup's left arm parried every thrust as if it had a life of its own.

'Well, suffering swordfish,' exclaimed Fishlegs. 'Hiccup is LEFT-HANDED.'

I would not have you think that this was a fight that Hiccup would be proud to look back upon NOW. For Hiccup would grow up to be a Master Swordsman, a Genius of the Art, and this fight by comparison with the extraordinary skill with which he fought later, was clumsy work, mostly defensive strokes.

And although I would love to say that Alvin the Treacherous was a brilliant swordfighter, the truth is that he was just so-so at the Art, preferring to poison his enemy's cup or bash him from behind with a rock to fighting him face to face.

But he was still much older, stronger and more experienced than Hiccup.

And while it might not have been the best fight Hiccup ever fought, it was certainly the one he would look back on with the most astonishment and pride.

For it was the first time in his life that Hiccup realised he was left-handed.

Imagine if you had spent the whole first part of your life trying to walk on your hands. The clumsiness of it, always falling over, always stumbling, always the last at everything. Imagine the joy of discovering that in fact you could walk on your feet after all.

That is what it felt like to Hiccup fighting with his left hand for the first time. So exhilarating was the feeling that he was even starting to enjoy himself.

Hiccup was helped by Toothless, who swooped down and attacked Alvin's head so that Alvin was constantly distracted.

'Unfair,' smiled Alvin. 'I never thought Grimbeard's Heir would stoop to TWO AGAINST ONE.'

The excitement made Hiccup overconfident and so he called out, 'Leave him to me, Toothless!'

'Leave him to you?' Fishlegs shouted up furiously. 'What do you mean, LEAVE HIM TO YOU??? CARRY ON, TOOTHLESS, AND THAT IS AN ORDER! This is REAL LIFE, Hiccup, not a Swordfighting at Sea lesson and you need all the help you can get...'

In fact, the practice from the Swordfighting at Sea lessons were a big help to Hiccup.

HOW TO SWORDFIGHT

Fig 1.

Knees bent, arms above head, relax and then swivel the hips, thrust forward and...

Fig 2.

... lunge!

The Piercing Lunge

The Destroyer's ← Defence

a. Raise sword above head,

b. Let out ear-splittingly ferocious yell.

c. Bring sword firmly forward as your feet leave the ground.

The Fighting-
Against-Superior-
Numbers-Manouvere

Remember to keep
your weight on the back
foot at all times. Be
careful not to remove
your own head with that axe.

The Confusing-the-enemy—
Bottoms-Up-Routine

Only for the very confident.

The shifting, moving ground of the treasure mound was rather similar to the movement of the deck at sea. Hiccup kept his balance more easily than Alvin, who continually staggered and lost his footing.

Nonetheless, it was soon clear that although Hiccup was enjoying himself he wasn't winning the fight, even with Toothless's help. With a grim smile on his lips, Alvin the Treacherous fought Hiccup back and back, eyes aglow with that red light, back to his old smooth self again.

'Come on, Hiccup,' he wheedled, 'don't be scared of your old pal, Treacherous. I wouldn't harm a hair,' *(swipe)* 'on your head,' *(swipe)*.

'Listen, Alvin,' urged Hiccup, as he parried each blow, 'I'm sure we can all get away safely if you forget about the treasure...'

'Oh, I will,' promised Alvin, 'just as soon as I've killed you, I will.'

'Look, Alvin,' reasoned Hiccup, 'it's never too late to change. You've still got a chance to live life differently, make friends, start a family...'

'Stop it,' said Alvin, 'you're making me laugh. *You* give *me* a second chance? That's really funny, that is. You're a heartbeat away from the abyss,

a mere child fighting a fully-grown man, and *you're* giving *me* second chances? It's too kind of you.'
He made a particularly violent lunge that Hiccup just managed to dodge, and very nearly lost his balance doing so.

'It's too late for me,' laughed Alvin. 'I'm rotten to the core and I like being rotten. The treasure has got me and I like being got.' He raised his sword way above his head as Hiccup clutched desperately at the shifting coins to steady himself.

'But I appreciate your concern,' said Alvin, bringing the sword down with such savage force that it would have cut Hiccup in half – if he had not spotted it coming and made one last leap out of the way.

So that the blow, instead of separating Hiccup into two pieces, caught Alvin completely off balance, and he stepped back on to the treasure mound behind, one on which they had not fought before…

… and the treasure unexpectedly reared up beneath him, as if it were alive.

18. GRIMBEARD THE GHASTLY'S FINAL SURPRISE

The entire mound reared up and shook itself, cups and jewels and swords and coins cascading down the sides like molten lava.

And something that looked like a big white rope reached out of the treasure and wound its way around Alvin's waist.

It wasn't a rope.

It was a singularly unattractive white tentacle that looked as if it were made out of a quivering piece of fat. The tentacle was dotted with small indentations out of which there oozed a disgusting whitey-grey sticky sludge that smelt indescribably awful.

Alvin shrieked in horror as the treasure dropped away to reveal the creature that had been sleeping underneath it, a creature they had awoken with their swordfight.

It was Grimbeard the Ghastly's last surprise, his FINAL booby trap.

He had left it there to guard the treasure, a monster that Hiccup had heard of in Legends,

but never seen before, and one that he sincerely hoped he would never, ever have to see again.

It was the same animal that surprised the little lost Deadly Nadder, the day before, if you remember, and it was called a Monstrous Strangulator.

A Strangulator was a gigantic Monster genetically related to dragons, octopuses, and snakes. It had tiny withered Dragon wings, and tiny crippled Dragon legs that were basically useless, as it heaved its great body through underground tunnels like a serpent, leaving a trail of gooey slime.

It had never seen daylight and was the colour of nothing. Its tentacles had obviously found a way up through to the upper caves of the Wild Dragon Cliffs, for it was transparent, and you could actually see the forms of unfortunate dragons it had eaten moving through its digestive system. Some, further down the Strangulator's great length, were lying quite still. Others that he had eaten more recently were jerking about, and one was trying to fly, trapped in the Monster's great throat.

The naturalist in Hiccup automatically identified the species – Monstrous Nightmare, Deadly Nadder, Common or Garden times three – making their slow

progress through the
Serpent's alimentary canal.

So small was the
Creature's brain in proportion to
its size, that it had difficulty in keeping
sensory track of all of its squirming tentacles
and they wandered about as if they had independent
lives of their own. The Creature had to concentrate
hard to make the tentacle that was holding Alvin move
very slowly up to its head so it could have a look at
him, unsure of what to make of this weird new animal.

'*Isss food?*' hissed the Serpent musingly to itself.

Hiccup practically cried with relief. For the
creature was speaking a dialect of Dragonese,
a very ancient form of it, but Dragonese nonetheless.

And Hiccup was of the opinion that if you could
talk to your killer, you were in with a chance.

Alvin struggled wildly and slashed at the great
squeezing tentacle with the Stormblade.

'*Tickle me with your prickle, would you?*' said
the Creature. '*Then I'll tickle you with mine...*'

And languidly, it dangled the tip of its tail in
front of Alvin's face.

Hiccup had seen such a tail on much smaller

197

animals. It was filled to the tip with a grass-green venom, pure as glass. There was a plunger a little way down, and the tip just had to penetrate its victim, the plunger go down, and it was goodnight sweet world, hello Valhalla.

Oh excellent, thought Hiccup to himself. *A* poisonous *Monstrous Strangulator. My favourite kind.*

Alvin fainted as soon as he set eyes on that deadly tail. He was frightened of needles.

So the Strangulator didn't even bother to inject him. It just swallowed him whole, alive, just as he was, Stormblade and all.

In fascinated horror, Hiccup watched the now awake and struggling form of Alvin travelling down the Strangulator's transparent throat.

So, thought Hiccup, *the Eater of Human Flesh is eaten himself. Isn't fate artistic?*

Sometimes it is harder to force yourself to stand still than it is to run away, but Hiccup knew that he wouldn't have a chance if he tried to escape. This animal was just too big. So Hiccup froze, in the hope that the Creature's eyesight was poor, like other beasts that lived solely underground.

Hiccup was probably right, but one of those

constantly-moving tentacles accidentally bumped into him, and as soon as it made contact with his warm body it automatically wrapped itself around Hiccup, and lifted him into the air.

'A Plan!' Fishlegs shouted out wildly from below. 'You need a Fiendishly Clever Plan!'

'Thank you, Fishlegs,' said Hiccup, his mind flicking about like a shrimp in a net, and trying to ignore the terrible squeezing around his chest. 'I'm aware of that... TOOTHLESS! Come up here!'

The tentacles were turning Hiccup over and over. Toothless flapped up, and hovered as close as he could. Hiccup shouted something into the little dragon's ear.

'That's a t-t-t-terrible plan,' moaned Toothless, shaking his head.

'Just do as you're told for ONCE in your life,' yelled Hiccup.

While the Creature remained unconscious of having caught anything he still stood a chance of escape. With his sword, he jabbed away at the sticky tentacle that was encircling his trunk and it seemed to be loosening...

Way down at the bottom of the treasure mound,

Fishlegs was frantically trying to be helpful.

In front of him, there lay a heavily bejewelled monstrosity of a sword. Despite the fact that it was nearly as big as himself, Fishlegs managed to pick it up from the floor. Purple in the face with the extraordinary effort, he lifted it high, high above his head, ready to launch it at the Creature's stomach…

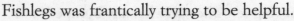

he
lifted
the sword
high, high
above his head...

Unfortunately the backwards momentum of the sword was so great that Fishlegs toppled ve-ry slowly backwards with it. There was a bronze shield on the floor behind him, and he landed on it with such force that he knocked himself out.

The noise of Fishlegs's head connecting with the shield caught the Creature's attention and light finally dawned in its dull eyes, which swam into focus on Hiccup. Its tentacles gripped strongly and escape became impossible.

'*More food?*' it mused to itself.

'NOT food!' Hiccup shouted out. 'I'm POISONOUS. Very, very POISONOUS!'

'*Poissonoussssss?*' hissed the Creature. '*It ss speakss and iss poisssonousss, is it? I'M poissssssonousssssss. Sssssssee?*'

And it waved the deadly plunger of its tail menacingly in front of Hiccup.

'*Don't like it when the food ssspeaks...*' whined the Creature to itself. '*Isss trickssssy when it ssspeaks... kill it quickly before it trickssss me...*'

It wrapped its tentacles a little tighter around Hiccup in order to suffocate him.

201

'This is all very interesting,' Hiccup managed to choke out, his eyes popping. 'So, how were you thinking of killing me, exactly?'

Gradually, the awful pressure on Hiccup's chest eased as the Strangulator considered this question.

'*Well,*' it said slowly, '*I wasssss thinking of sssssssqueezing you to death...*'

'I only ask,' said Hiccup, gasping for air, 'because I was recently nearly swallowed by a Seadragonus Giganticus Maximus, who said that you Undergrounders were very primitive animals, poorly armed, and only capable of basic forms of killing, such as strangulation.'

The Creature stopped squeezing entirely.

'*That'ssss very rude,*' it hissed eventually, rather hurt. '*What isssss thissss Giganti-Maxi-thingy anyway?*'

'Release your tentacles a bit,' said Hiccup, 'and I'll tell you.'

'*OK,*' said the Strangulator, '*but no tricksssing or I'll get crossssss.*'

Slowly the Creature unwound its tentacles, leaving them only loosely wrapped about the boy. Hiccup took in great relieved gulps of air.

'A Seadragonus Giganticus Maximus,' Hiccup continued, 'is a gigantic, scary killing machine as big as a mountain...'

'*I'm big...*' the Creature pointed out.

'It has at least three ways of killing,' said Hiccup. 'It can rip you to pieces with its talons, bite you to bits with its teeth, or fry you to a frazzle with its fire.'

'*I can do that...*' said the Creature, less certainly.

'No you can't,' said Hiccup. 'You haven't got any talons, teeth, or fire.'

'*Sssssso I haven't,*' said the Strangulator, very disappointed. '*But I can sssssssqueeze you to death...*' He brightened up and began to wrap his tentacles around Hiccup again.

'So OLD-FASHIONED!' shrieked Hiccup hurriedly. 'What about the POISON? That's the most modern method of killing around. A Seadragonus Giganticus Maximus hasn't got any poison...'

'*Hassssssssn't it?*' asked the Creature delightedly.

'No, it hasn't,' said Hiccup. 'I'm very curious to see how one of these fancy new poisons works.'

'*It'sssss not a niccccccce way to go,*' warned the Creature.

It pointed the sharp needle of its tail straight at Hiccup's heart.

Suddenly, Toothless flew into the Strangulator's field of vison. The Creature lost concentration for a second as the little dragon zoomed up and down right in front of its eyes. By the time it had co-ordinated its tentacles enough to frighten Toothless away, the Strangulator was very, very cross.

'I told you, no trickssssssing!' it hissed, with venom in its voice. *'Thisssss will shut you up...'*

Fishlegs came back into consciousness just in time to see the Strangulator inject the whole tail's-worth of green poison, enough to kill the entire population of Rome, into the flesh beneath Hiccup's shirt.

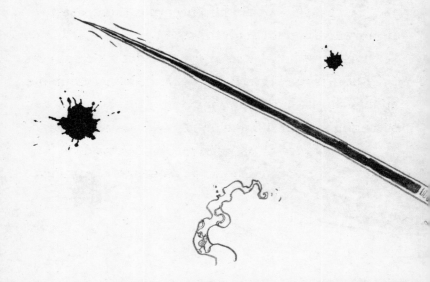

19. THE HEIR TO GRIMBEARD THE GHASTLY

'So,' chatted Hiccup, 'while we're waiting for this poison to take effect, why don't you tell me how it works?'

'*Well,*' crowed the Strangulator, '*you will lose control of your tentaclesss ass they sssstart to sssstiffen...*'

'I can feel a sort of tingling in my feet, like pins and needles,' admitted Hiccup.

The Strangulator's own tentacles were leaping about wildly, as stiff as boards.

'*The poissson turnsss sssome victimsss green before they die...*' hissed the Strangulator gleefully.

'Is it just me,' said Hiccup, 'or is there a sort of greenish tinge to my left arm?'

There wasn't. It was as white and freckled as ever.

But a strange green cloud was building within the Strangulator's transparent body, gradually obscuring the unfortunate dragons he was digesting.

'*... and then as the poissson reaches the head,*' continued the Strangulator, '*the nervoussss ssysssstem* sssssimply explodesss...'

He looked at Hiccup hopefully.

Nothing seemed to be happening.

'That'sss funny,' said the Strangulator. '
It doesn't sssseem to be working...'

'Maybe some people take longer,' said Hiccup
reassuringly. 'You're looking a little peaky yourself,
maybe you should lie down.'

The Strangulator looked down at itself. The green
cloud had now blown into every crook and cranny of
its body, and was finally approaching its tiny brain...

'AAAAAAAAAAAAAAAAAGH!'

screeched the Strangulator.

The nervous system of the Strangulator simply
exploded.

All of its electric circuits lit up like light bulbs.
It thrashed around like a mad thing, knocking out
great chunks of rock from the sides of the cave and
sending treasure flying through the air in all directions.

Fishlegs hid himself underneath an overhanging
rock in order not to be hit by the whirling coils.
Toothless crawled into a crevice in the ceiling. For
about a minute and a half the Strangulator threw

itself wildly off the walls of the cavern, screeching a strange primeval agonised shriek. Then all of its tentacles stood out straight and stiff and it fell to the ground.

The Strangulator jerked a few more times in agony. Its tail with the dangerous tip lashed ferociously for a moment or two. And then all was silence in the Great Cavern. Huge clouds of dust gradually dispersed.

Fishlegs crawled out of his hiding-place.

He scrambled over slimy rock-falls, slimy treasure, and even slimier coils of Strangulator, looking for Hiccup.

Hiccup was dazed but alive. He'd had a tidal wave of a ride, thrown this way and that way until his teeth rattled. But the great coils of the tentacle wrapped around his body had cushioned him from any hurt.

He beamed at Fishlegs and Toothless.

'That was one STUPID Monster,' he said.

'How did you DO it? How did you DO it?' asked Fishlegs again and again in amazement as he and Toothless unwound the tentacle from Hiccup's body.

For answer, Hiccup lifted up his shirt, and there, wrapped around his chest, was the very tip of the tentacle... and in the gelatinous transparent flesh of it was a giant needle puncture mark, with the green poison clearly visible coursing underneath the skin.

What Hiccup had done was to pull his shirt OVER the end of the tentacle while Toothless was distracting the Creature. The Strangulator had so lost sensory contact with the ends of its tentacles that it did not realise that it was in fact injecting ITSELF under the white material of Hiccup's shirt.

'That particular plan,' said Fishlegs at last, 'required a Fiendish Amount of LUCK.'

'It WAS lucky,' admitted Hiccup happily, 'but we're ALIVE, aren't we?'

Fishlegs grinned back at him and Toothless did three back somersaults in the air and a congratulatory cock-a-doodle-doo.

'And that swordfighting. Where did THAT come from? You've always been grim at swordfighting.'

'Swapped hands,' mumbled Hiccup, beaming but a bit embarrassed.

'A left-handed genius who single-handedly defeated Alvin the Treacherous AND a Monstrous Strangulator,' gloated Fishlegs. 'This is going to look so GOOD when we tell everybody back home. I just can't WAIT to see the look on Snotlout's face when he sets eyes on this treasure. It makes that poxy little box he dug up on the Isle of the Skullions look pretty measly.'

'Yeeees,' said Hiccup slowly. 'but we ARE still trapped in an inaccessible underground cavern, aren't we? We have to GET OUT OF HERE first.'

Fishlegs's face fell. 'So we do,' he admitted. 'But the Creature must have some way from this cavern up to the caves in the Wild Dragon Cliff... I mean, look at those dragons in his digestive system, he must have been feeding off the Dragon Nursery for years. All we have to do is go through these Caliban Caves and—'

'N-n-no,' said Toothless firmly. 'T-t-toothless knows. Toothless grow up here. Other C-c-creatures in there much bigger and b-b-badder than that one...'

'OK then,' said Hiccup. 'We go back the way we came. Let's hope that door still opens.'

The door did still open.

As they were opening it, Hiccup noticed a piece of paper nailed on their side of it.

It was a letter.

It was written in the same scrawly handwriting as Grimbeard's riddle, and it was addressed to the 'TRUE HEIR OF GRIMBEARD THE GHASTLY'.

Hiccup took the letter off the nail and read it.

DEAR HEIR,

(said the letter)

I have had a glorious Viking life. But now I am an old, old man I find I am not so happy with my fifty years of rollicking and robbery, fighting and fresh air. I wonder if I might have run things differently. This treasure for instance. The Sagas will tell you that the stealing of it was my **Most Magnificent Moment.**

But since then, it has been tearing my once-happy band of burglars apart with **GREED** and **LUST FOR POWER.**

We are just not ready to look after this treasure. So I have decided to get rid of it.

I know that there will be men who will hear of the Legend of the Treasure and come looking for it, and for them I have buried a small chest on the Isle of the Skullions as a decoy, so that they will think that the hunt ends there. I have hidden the

REAL TREASURE

deep, deep in this underground cavern. It has taken many many months for my dragons to swim down here with it. It is guarded by water one way and the Caliban Caves the other. I have placed an infant Strangulator in the Cavern who shall grow in time to be a terrible Guardian indeed. I dream of a time in the future when men will be able to own such beautiful and dangerous things and use them wisely.

I dream of an Heir who shall be a Dragon-Whisperer, a Swordfighter, a Man who talks with Monsters and who will harness the power of Thor's thunder itself... This Heir will come and he will find my treasure. I give it to him freely, all of it, and he shall know what to do with it.

I wish you good luck and a nice strong wind,

Grimbeard the Ghastly

P.S. I hope you have a dragon with you, he can help you to the surface. Otherwise I am afraid you are done for.

'Maybe Grimbeard the Ghastly wasn't so bad
after all...' said Hiccup slowly.

'There you are,' said Fishlegs, who was reading
over Hiccup's shoulder. 'He said it was YOUR
treasure, to do as you liked with.'

Hiccup sighed. He thought of the greedy
look in Stoick's eyes when he held the Stormblade. He
thought of Baggybum and Stoick arguing over
the treasure chest.

'Yes,' said Hiccup, 'and I DO know what to
do with it.'

He picked up a piece of charcoal from the cavern floor, wrote some words on the bottom of the letter, and pinned it back on the door.

'STILL... NOT... READY...' read Fishlegs.

Fishlegs hurried after Hiccup, who was now looking at the cavern's exit hole to the sea, thinking hard.

'What do you mean, *still not ready?*' demanded Fishlegs.

'I mean,' said Hiccup, 'that the treasure is staying right here. That this is our SECRET and we tell NOBODY. If we get out of here alive, we just say we washed up on the shore a couple of beaches down, no mention of the existence of this cavern, nothing.'

'You CANNOT BE SERIOUS,' said Fishlegs. 'We could be HEROES here, and besides, if we don't tell everybody what happened, they'll all go on thinking that Snotlout is the True Heir to the Hairy Hooligans.'

Hiccup looked miserable. 'I guess that's right,' he said. 'But then if I really *am* the True Heir, I have to do what I think is the right thing for the Tribe, don't I? And this is definitely the right thing. That treasure is Bad Trouble.'

Hiccup would not change his mind.

'Let's just concentrate on getting back home,' he said.

It took Hiccup two or three hours of hard thinking to work out how to use one dragon to get himself and Fishlegs up through hundreds of feet of water and back to the surface without drowning.

The solution is quite simple, if you ever find yourself in a similarly tricky situation.

A dragon's breath, even when it exhales, is composed almost entirely of pure oxygen. It is this that makes it so very flammable. All they needed to do was to rise to the surface (slowly, so as not to get the bends) with Toothless swimming beside them and occasionally blowing into their noses when they ran out of breath.

A dragon never runs out of breath because just below its horns it has a fully working set of gills. As soon as it enters the sea it can shut off its lungs and get its oxygen from the water rather than the air.

Hiccup and Fishlegs resurfaced after about ten minutes. There was plenty of debris floating around, because they were not far from where the *Lucky Thirteen* had made its final journey to the bottom of the ocean. The boys each got hold of one end of an oar, and steered their way around the corner to where there was a beach to land on.

Fishlegs tried to persuade Hiccup to change his mind all the way home.

At last he said in exasperation, 'You're NEVER going to be a Hero with this attitude. How *can* you be with no one to cheer, no one to clap?'

'OK then,' Hiccup sighed. 'I'll never be a Hero. All I know is that I'm supposed to be the Future Leader of this Tribe and I want there to be a Tribe left to lead. And that seems more important to me than being a Hero.'

They staggered through the heather towards

the Hooligan Village, which was strangely silent
and deserted. No smoke curled from the rooftops,
no children quarrelled in the streets, no dragons were
fighting in the thatch.

'Please, please, good god Woden,' prayed
Hiccup, 'PLEASE let everybody be alive.'

Everybody *was* alive.

Miraculously, no one had drowned during the
sinking of the *Lucky Thirteen*.

The Hooligans sailed the heavily overloaded
Hammerhead back to Berk, with the Outcasts tied
up as their prisoners.

With typical generosity, they set the Outcasts free.

I fear the Outcasts were not as grateful as
they should have been, and this would not be the
last the Hooligans would see of these vicious people.
For the moment, however, they returned to the
Outcast Lands humiliated, unarmed, and with
a hunger for revenge.

The Hooligans were not in much better shape
themselves. They were a hardy race, and drowning
was an occupational hazard, but the loss of the only son
of the Chief was a big blow, whether he was
the Heir or not.

Stoick sat for an hour at the edge of the sea.
As soon as Snotlout's treasure had disappeared
beneath the waves it had lost its magic for him.
He kept on seeing in his mind's eye his son, Hiccup,
standing on the deck of the *Lucky Thirteen*, saying,
'I AM THE HEIR TO STOICK THE VAST.'

He tore out his golden earrings, and threw
them into the ocean. And then he went home and
sat in front of his shrine to Woden.

So this was why, when Fishlegs, Hiccup and
Toothless came stumbling and limping into the
Hooligan Village, everyone had locked themselves
indoors, the shutters were shut up, doors were closed,
fires were unlit.

It was only a chance that the wooden window
had blown open in Gobber the Belch's home. He
went to close it, and happened to spot the bedraggled
friends lurching along... And then he let out a great
bellow of, 'They're ALIVE!!!'

The shout went from house to house like
watch fires lighting from hill to hill, and the Hairy
Hooligans rushed out of their front doors like a crowd
of jubilant sea-elephants, and they swooped on the
three companions and lifted them on to their muscly

shoulders with great happy shouts of, 'They're
ALIVE! They're ALIVE! THEY'RE ALIVE!
THEY'RE ALIVE!'

Snotlout was already furious to find that people
had been more concerned about mourning Hiccup and
Fishlegs than congratulating HIM on being the Hero
of the Hour on the Isle of the Skullions.

Imagine how cross he was to run out of his house
in curiosity at the commotion, to find himself barged
out of the way by Gobber the Belch and Nobber
Nobrains, and practically trampled into the ground
by a clapping mob carrying Hiccup shoulder high
through the Village.

Hiccup, who was quite clearly, yet again,
NOT dead, NOT drowned, NOT safely out of the way.

The happy Hooligans reached the door of
their Chieftain's house and banged on it crying,
'Open up, open up, they're alive, they're alive!'

Stoick the Vast lifted his great hairy head as
if he was dreaming, staggered to the door, and there,
on the doorstep, was HIS SON, Hiccup.

Stoick the Vast, Terror of the Seas, Most High
Ruler of the Hairy Hooligans, O Hear his Name and
Tremble, Ugh, Ugh, picked up his son and hugged

him, while the crowd cheered and cheered.

And that was how Toothless found and lost a marvellous treasure all in the space of an afternoon...

... And how Hiccup finally got himself a sword and learnt how to use it...

... And how Fishlegs discovered that you don't always have to be a Hero to get a Hero's Welcome.

EPILOGUE BY HICCUP

A few months afterwards, I had a dream.

It was a dream about shipwrecks, perhaps because I had been doing a lot of that lately. The ship was called the *Endless Journey,* and just before it disappeared beneath the waves, the ferocious looking captain, who had a strange smile on his face, threw a sword up, up, into the air. It spun end to end over the waves, through the atmosphere and into space and stars and neverending time, where, to my surprise, my own left hand sprang out of its own accord and caught it.

As soon as I awoke, I got up and brought out that uninspiring sword that Toothless had picked for me in the cavern of the Treasure, the one with which I had fought Alvin the Treacherous. I turned it over and over, and inspected the dull little object for quite half an hour. And eventually I found that by twisting and twisting it, the knob at the end fell off and there was a small piece of paper rolled up in a little hollowed-out compartment inside. A small fragment of paper on which was written the following words:

The Last Will and Testament
~of~
Grimbeard the Ghastly

I leave to my True Heir,
this my favourite sword.
Because the Stormblade
always lunged a little to
the left.
And the Best is not always
the most Obvious.

Yours,
In the hope that
you will make a better
Leader than
I was,

G.G.

Now I am an old, old man, the same age as
Grimbeard the Ghastly when he got his dragons to
swim down to the cavern with the treasure. Toothless
and Fishlegs and I have kept the secret of what really
happened on that terrible day all those years ago...

But because I am writing my memoirs I find
I have to write it down, as it is such an important
part of my journey to becoming a Hero. Even though I
know I will never be able to show it to anyone of
my own time.

As soon as I have finished writing these papers,
I shall lock them in a box. I shall throw that box
into the sea.

And I shall throw it hoping, like Grimbeard the
Ghastly, that some day it may be found by someone
who will be a better Leader than I have been.

Someone living way, way, in the future, in times
more civilised than those in which I have lived, where
men can own beautiful and dangerous things and use
them wisely.

Surely that would be the last Hiccup would see of that wicked villain, **Alvin the Treacherous?**

His grim hook sank to the bottom of the ocean with the wreck of the **Lucky Thirteen.** *He himself was last seen struggling in the throat of a Monstrous Strangulator in an inaccessible cavern deep, deep underground.*

Nobody could get out of that situation alive.

Or could they???

Look out for the next volume of Hiccup's memoirs, **How to Speak Dragonese**

This is Cressida, age 9, writing on the island.

Cressida Cowell grew up in London and
on a small, uninhabited island off the west
coast of Scotland where she spent her time
writing stories, fishing for things to eat,
and exploring the island looking for dragons.
She was convinced that there were dragons
living on the island, and has been
fascinated by them ever since.

www.cressidacowell.com

HOWDEEDOODEETHERE!

For your latest news on all things dragon and Cressida Cowell please follow:

 @cressidacowellauthor

 @cressidacowell

 facebook.com/
cressidacowellauthor

 Toodleoon for now...

'Exciting adventures, great characters and
plenty of jokes and funny drawings make
Hiccup's adventures some of our favourite books.'
TBK Magazine

'Cowell's Dragon books are proper
modern classics.' **Sunday Express**

'This series is one of the greatest ever
written for those between eight and twelve.
Buy them all and your holidays will be blessed
with perfect peace.' **The New Statesman**

'Cowell has crafted a modern classic ...
every bit as consuming and deep as Harry's
in Hogwarts ... And so the fight – part Doctor Who,
part biblical epic – begins.' **The BIG Issue**

'One of the greatest pleasures of children's
literature. Staggeringly clever and funny
mash of Beowulf and Potter, with a truly unusual
and "heroic" hero.' **Peter Florence**

'Hilarious and wise, it's never
predictable, brilliantly illustrated and
always delightful.' **The Times**

'Rollicking fun' **Guardian**

CRESSIDA COWELL
HOW TO TRAIN YOUR DRAGON

ALSO AVAILABLE IN AUDIO
READ BY THE AWARD-WINNING ACTOR
DAVID TENNANT

'If you have six to twelve-year-olds, and you don't know
about David Tennant's readings of Cressida Cowell's
How to Train Your Dragon series, you don't deserve to be
a parent ... Simply the best of kids' audio-listening,
and just as much fun for parents.'
The Times

'This kept us all laughing on the edge of our seats.'
Independent on Sunday

AUDIO
Read by
DAVID
TENNANT

Want to listen to an extract?
https://soundcloud.com/hachettekids

READ HICCUP'S GUIDE
TO DRAGON SPECIES ...

Full of dragon profiles and tips on how to ride and
train them ... a **MUST READ** for anyone who wants
to know more about dragons.

The WIZARDS of ONCE

Once there Was Magic...

This is the story of a young boy Wizard, and a young girl Warrior, who have been taught to hate each other like poison.

#wizardsofonce